The Husband Heist

The Dainty Devils
Book 3

By Alyxandra Harvey

DRAGONBLADE
PUBLISHING, INC.

ARE YOU SIGNED UP FOR DRAGONBLADE'S BLOG?

You'll get the latest news and information on exclusive giveaways, exclusive excerpts, coming releases, sales, free books, cover reveals and more.

Check out our complete list of authors, too!

No spam, no junk. That's a promise!

Sign Up Here

www.dragonbladepublishing.com

Dearest Reader;

Thank you for your support of a small press. At Dragonblade Publishing, we strive to bring you the highest quality Historical Romance from some of the best authors in the business. Without your support, there is no 'us', so we sincerely hope you adore these stories and find some new favorite authors along the way.

Happy Reading!

CEO, Dragonblade Publishing

Additional Dragonblade books by Author Alyxandra Harvey

The Dainty Devils Series
The Duchess Games (Book 1)
The Countess Caper (Book 2)
The Husband Heist (Book 3)

The Cinderella Society Series
How to Marry an Earl (Book 1)
How to Marry a Duke (Book 2)
How to Marry a Viscount (Book 3)

Chapter One

Mayfair, London, 1805

B Y THE TIME Lady Summer realized that beards itched like the devil, it was too late to turn back.

As a duke's sister, she was accustomed to a certain degree of luxury. She knew gold candlesticks and diamond hairpins, silk gloves and velvet reticules. She knew dancing under honey-scented candles dripping from elaborate chandeliers and the best champagne bubbling in fluted crystal glasses.

This was so much better.

Even with the itchy beard currently glued to her face.

At thirty-three years old, with every privilege, she honestly could not think of when she had last been happier. She wasn't dancing on the arm of a handsome gentleman, or laughing with friends, showing off a new dress, winning a hand of cards. She was sneaking into a private art society with less-than-honorable intentions. And she could have giggled with pure joy.

Except that art thieves did not giggle.

Nor did Lady Summer.

Oh, but it was there, fizzing in the back of her throat like that champagne she was not drinking.

The Mayfair Art Collectors Society would not know what hit them.

Preferably, it would be her.

If not tonight, then very, very soon.

Right in the face.

Someone was playing the pianoforte, and the music floated through the house, punctuated with shouts of laughter. This might look like any other grand house, with polished parquet floors, gilded sconces, wallpaper patterned to look like lavish damask. Only instead of portraits of ancestors and spaniels and enormous cows watching from every corner, there were marbles from Greece, friezes from Italy, art from Venice. Sketches, faded oil paintings, watercolors.

A collection of art and sculptures from gentlemen on their Grand Tours and from the tours of their grandfathers, all displayed like so many war trophies.

She'd bring them a war, if that's what they wanted.

Aunt Georgie would be avenged.

Tonight, they drank their smuggled French brandy and smoked their cheroots and bemoaned that the Grand Tours of their sons could not include the brothels and galleries of France. Only the brave or the very stupid would traipse about the Continent with Napoleon on their heels. And the Collectors were not brave. She would like to have said they were indeed stupid, but they weren't that either. What they were was arrogant, and entitled, and overdue for a comeuppance.

On behalf of Lady Georgette Deveraux, Dowager Countess Sutherland, Summer was about to complete the first step of the plan meant to deliver that comeuppance.

In her itchy beard.

Damnation, how did people choose to walk around with a ferret wrapped around their chin? To be fair, the stage glue was probably the culprit behind the itching. Still. Beards were certainly more bother than she would have assumed.

Worth it, though.

Completely, *completely* worth it as she walked by Lord Bailey and he did not even glance at her. Just last week he stared rather fixedly at her cleavage as if it might hold the answers to the universe.

But the Mayfair Art Collectors Society did not admit women to their society. Nor their house. At least not tonight. Once a year they held an event meant to dazzle the *ton*, a sort of art exhibition and ball rolled into one. Members displayed their beloved art in one place for one night only. Participation was mandatory. Which meant Lord Glass would be in attendance, and he was high on the list of members she very, very much wanted to punch in the face.

Justice was taking far too long.

Hence, Lady Summer had traded her diamonds for a false beard.

She passed pedestals crowned with the blank-eyed busts of ancient Romans, paintings interspersed between them, reaching the ceiling. They were mostly beiges and grays and faded greens. The original artists would have been appalled. They certainly had not chosen colors that brought to mind dirty dishwasher. But the years took their toll. Their due.

As her mother insisted on reminding her.

Spinsters in their thirties were forgettable, duke's sisters or not. Even when they still carried the nickname of *the Diamond*. They ought to be married and carrying on the lineage of some much-vaulted English aristocracy family instead.

Again, this was so much better.

She would happily be a spinster until the day she died, and not just to spite her mother. She missed her twin brother Callum, but he had married and had a duchess to run his house now. Summer adored Cat, even if Summer's mother refused to acknowledge her. Dukes did not often marry girls from fishing villages. Callum had even finally managed to drown out their mother's voice in his head insisting that he had to be perfect, a marble statue of a duke.

Summer left him in good hands.

But, she had to admit, it left her feeling rather aimless. Floating through Mayfair as the Diamond was growing rather tedious. She was expected to care about every change in fashion, about other people's guest lists, and furniture.

She did not.

She was expected to give her opinion. Worse, she was also constantly asked to make decisions about the wallpaper in other people's bedrooms and parlors.

Until Aunt Georgie and the need for retribution. Summer finally had what she needed: adventure, purpose. Three women with questionable talents and principles at her back.

So there, Mother.

Right. Arguing with her mother, however natural and reasonable, was not particularly helpful at the moment.

And anyway, this was not the full collection, nor the exhibition. This was just a test. A test of spirit glue and beards and whatever it was Beatrix did when she gathered information. She was a master of disguise, of disappearing. This would have been her job, but Summer knew the *ton*, knew their quirks, and knew art. She would remember everything she saw and be able to sketch it out later, right down to the smallest detail.

For the proper exhibition, the most noteworthy and most expensive items would be curated in the repurposed conservatory.

Locked down. Protected by puzzles and burly guards and pistols.

A gentleman glanced at her as he stumbled past. She reminded herself not to freeze up. She was pretending to be an earl's son, and she belonged here. He only snorted at the slight young man with the patchy beard before clapping him roughly on the shoulder. Summer teetered dangerously. "Drink up!" he barked, shoving his half-empty glass at her. She took it before it collided with her chest.

She'd chosen a later hour when they would be befuddled with drink. They might be a society of collectors, but it was also the start of the Season in London. There wasn't an aristocrat sober from here to the Thames.

When he wandered away, she hid a grin, and relief and a

renewed bolt of confidence moved through her. She could learn to love this. The thrill of nerves, the prickle of awareness across the back of her neck. Better than any assignations. Which said more than she liked about the current quality of her assignations.

Never mind that. She had breeched the walls of the Mayfair Art Collectors Society. She was inside the belly of the beast. And she intended to cause them no end of indigestion.

The conservatory had polished floors, curtains at the windows, sconces in the wall. Skylights up above, like the Royal Art Exhibition, to better let light inside to showcase art. Paintings could be hung all the way to the ceiling and still be relatively visible, all without damaging the canvases with too much direct sun. Which would be more helpful if the exhibition was held during the daylight hours. But alas. Being reasonable was nowhere near as necessary as being dramatic.

Better yet, skylights were a vulnerable point of entry.

That excitement again, piercing through the sameness of her life.

She studied the skylights for another moment, memorizing the shape of them. The moon had wandered somewhere else, but the oil lamps were lit. There was a picture rail, hooks, and a veritable forest of pedestals waiting for sculptures and vases. There were items on display, but nothing truly unique yet.

This is just the first step, she reminded herself. A bit of reconnaissance. Preparation.

And she was prepared.

If she was caught snooping: act the drunk lord. She'd had enough experience dealing with them to know how they behaved. A blurring blink of the eye, a stagger. A spill of any nearby drink, preferably on something valuable. She would be forgotten, for one furious moment. Enough to run away. Far away.

If she was recognized: play it off as a lark. A dare for the mildly notorious Lady Summer. Bring up her brother, the Duke of Tremaine. A lot.

She would rather not sacrifice her reputation—it came in far too useful. Lady Summer had already been invited to the Collectors' masquerade gala, after all. Her love of art was already well known. She could not afford to be turned away at the door. A curiosity, a story to tell, was perfectly fine. A true scandal, less so.

For now.

All to say: she was prepared for almost anything. Being recognized, being caught red-handed, forced to join a drinking game with port, which she despised. Play at cards, ogle a courtesan. She'd even memorized a limerick for the occasion. Drunken second sons of earls recited racy limericks, didn't they?

She had not, however, prepared for Eliot Howard, Earl of Blackpool.

In fact, she would have been less surprised if a family of badgers paraded past, dancing a jig while wearing matching tricorn hats.

If Summer had a nemesis, it wasn't her mother. It wasn't the girl who had bested her in a horse race when she was twelve. It wasn't even the odious Revenue Man in the village back home who looked down his London nose at all things Cornish.

It was Blackpool.

Why did a single glance at him do things to her insides? Nice things.

She would not have it. He was entirely too accustomed to adoration as it was. Between the confidence lent to him from his father's title and the dark eyes and dark hair from his Colonial French-Micmac mother, he was a menace to female society. All society. Women were certainly not the only ones to notice him.

You would have to be dead not to notice him.

Everything about him exuded charm and sensuality. Craving. Temptation. Add the self-deprecating smile and the knowing lift of an eyebrow and honestly, he ought to come with a warning. Bugles of war sounding as he prowled through a room, stays and too-tight lacings and other unmentionables dropping to the floor behind him.

It was her duty to needle him. As the sister of his oldest friend. As a woman.

Why was he even here? He was not a Collector. He didn't give a fig for art or sculptures or societies that excluded women. How would he secure his daily requirement of flattery? Or tiny sighs, and shy smiles behind fans.

She took it back. He absolutely was a collector—but of nothing useful.

He could not see her. Not that he would recognize her. The beard, for one. But he was insufferable, always poking at her, teasing her. Issuing ridiculous challenges.

They had competed over every little thing for over a decade. He was the only one who ever dared vie against her. Even winning, sometimes.

At least half the time.

It was as infuriating as it was refreshing.

But if he caught her here, he would hound her for an explanation until she hit him over the head with a two-thousand-year-old vase.

It was a bit harder to be a successful art thief when you were running from the law for murder.

She slipped further inside the ballroom, ducking her head slightly. He had no reason to look her way, to notice her, to find her in any way familiar. There was only one other person in the room, and he was currently sitting propped against the wall, snoring with a full glass of wine balanced on his knee. A talent, that.

She kept her back to the door, her eyes on the various points of display. Would Aunt Georgie's collection be locked behind glass doors, under a bell jar, in a locked case, on a pedestal?

Regardless, it would be back in her drawing room by the end of the week.

She straightened her shoulders, feeling bolder.

Until that voice, usually drawling her name, snapped in her ear, laced with something else entirely.

"What the bloody hell are you doing here?"

Chapter Two

*B*OLLOCKS.

Summer waited a moment, hoping against hope that Blackpool had mistaken her for someone else. That he was talking to the unconscious man against the wall.

"Summer, why are you dressed like that?" he bit out.

How had he even seen her? Recognized her? She turned her head sharply. "Hush."

He blinked down at her. "I retract the question."

"I highly doubt that."

"A follow-up question, then." The snap in his voice turned to a purr.

Damn the man. He simply could not help himself. "Go away, Blackpool."

"Not until you tell what you are wearing on your face." A flicker of amusement, curiosity, behind something that burned with more intensity than the moment deserved. Something she responded to, despite herself.

"It's a beard," she said primly. Her governess would have been proud, twenty years later. It was her exact tone, trotted out when Summer asked too many questions or stole the raspberry scones from the kitchen before they had properly cooled. Or mocked her mother. "Obviously."

"Obviously." When she shifted away, ready to slip out, his

hand closed around her elbow. Not hard, but still unbreakable. "Oh, I don't think so," he added silkily.

She did not have the time to examine why something inside her went hot and liquid. Nor the inclination.

No inclination whatsoever.

This was Blackpool. Irritating to the extreme. But also unfairly and ridiculously handsome, with those strangely delicate features, but also a strong jaw, a slash of dark eyebrows. She could recognize that and still want to poke him with a sharp stick. She contained multitudes.

"I'll ask again, what are you doing here, Summer?"

"And I'll say again: go away, Blackpool."

He still had not released her arm. "It's not safe here."

"At a men's club?" she asked incredulously. "I know how to handle *men*."

"I am aware."

"What's that supposed to mean?" She'd been raised in Mayfair. She knew how to flirt her way out of a thousand dangers. A weapon was a weapon. And until she figured out a way to hide more than a sharp hairpin in her chignon, it would have to suffice. Although a sword would have been nice.

"This isn't just any men's club."

"I know where I am, Blackpool. Do you suppose this costume is an accident?"

"I can't begin to imagine." He swore under his breath. "Damn it all, did Aunt Georgie put you up to this?"

She tossed him a careless smile, changing tactics. Perhaps it would be best to throw him off guard, to make light. To be *Lady Summer. The Diamond.*

He was not convinced.

"I don't think so." This against her most charming, flirtatious smile. The one she was fairly certain had saved her from prison that one time. And being tossed into the Thames that other time.

She huffed out a sigh. "I don't have time for this."

He smirked that damnable smirk. "While I happen to have all

the time in the world. Did she send you?"

She shrugged one shoulder, obstinate to the core.

"I told her I would take care of it," he muttered.

She sniffed. "You were taking too long. Your services are no longer required."

"Like *hell*."

She glanced over her shoulder at the open doorway, the flickering shadows of the sconces. "Do *not* draw attention to me, you lummox."

"As if you need my help with that," he muttered. He prowled the room, eyebrows lowered. "What are you even doing here?" he asked. "Her collection is not here yet."

"We know that."

"We?"

Blast. She should not be giving him any more ammunition than he already had.

"If it's not just her art, then what?" He continued to walk the perimeter, disdaining antiquities, flicking his hand at empty pedestals, tracking her reaction. "This vase? That painting?"

"No, of course—Don't!"

Too late.

He caught the vase as it teetered, rescuing it before it crashed to the floor, but that wasn't her worry. In his cavalier stroll, he'd stepped on a trick floorboard. She knew they were scattered throughout the room, but she had not had the opportunity to map them out.

He'd found the first one. With his big, stupid foot.

The squeak was unnaturally loud.

"What the devil?" Blackpool froze.

He took another step, but it was too late. Every move he made had the floor singing like a chorus of birds at dawn. Loudly. She had heard of floors like this in Japan, set around bedrooms to warn of intruders. An entire ballroom set up this way would have been deafening when empty but useless when filled with footmen rushing to and fro with trays of refreshments, with dancers and the music of an orchestra.

The gala was still a week away, and they were not yet on high alert.

Still. Some knowledge was better than none.

Options, options. She could hear Beatrix's no-nonsense lecture in her head. *Use it. Gather information. Every mishap is an opportunity.*

If nothing else, she would have firsthand experience of their security setup, how fast they responded.

Which was to say: fast.

Blackpool was still frowning with bewilderment when the first guard joined them. He was tall and very wide and did not appear to have a sense of humor stored anywhere on his person. And if he was a Collector, she would eat her beard.

There had to be wires under those floorboards connected to bells downstairs, like the bells she rang at home for tea. They'd have to disable those at the very least. A job for Beatrix. Maggie would handle the skylight. As she did handstands on a horse's back at Astley's Amphitheatre on a regular basis, it would prove little challenge for her.

Blackpool's eyebrow rose. He knew hired muscle when he saw it. She saw the shift in him, from vigilant to relaxed, charming. Without a care to his name. A rake, through and through. "Something's wrong with your floor," he said cheerfully.

"What are you doing in here?" The guard scowled.

Both of Blackpool's eyebrows rose this time. "Having a drink, seeing some art. What else does one do here?"

That was the real question.

Sir Muscles eyed Summer suspiciously. "I don't know you."

Summer prayed she could drop her voice believably. Another test. No time like the present, with two men watching her distrustfully. "Don't know you, either," she returned, just this side of belligerently. Her brother, the very proper duke, had never been belligerent a day in his life. Blackpool, however, could take credit for her experience of it. He had been most unbearable the summer he was fifteen. To her, if no one else.

Sir Muscles snorted.

"My cousin," Blackpool said easily, though his fingers tightened on the back of her coat when she tried to move away. "My uncle sent him to Town for some polish. You know how it is."

"Eh?" The man in the corner started violently, spilling his wine.

The house butler marched inside, as if summoned by the drunken yelp. He sighed down at the man, then jolted when he noticed the guard. "Not again."

"Nothing for you to worry about."

"I can't run a house like this. Some of these items are irreplaceable!"

Interesting.

She tucked the tiny argument away for later. Blackpool was very close to her—she could feel him looming at her back. The butler turned to them both. He seemed too tense, too aware, to be convinced by her beard. And if he was anything like the butlers manning her brother's various houses, she knew just how to distract him. Disorder, unpleasantness. A stain on the damask cushions.

"Too much wine," Summer slurred suddenly, clutching her stomach.

"Not in here!" the butler snapped.

Blackpool had no option but to let her go. She darted away, making noises in the back of her throat. Disgusting noises. The butler all but leapt out of her way.

She was down the hall and out the front door before Blackpool could catch her.

Chapter Three

THERE WAS A woman hanging upside down from the ceiling.

It was past midnight, and a woman dangled from aerial silks inside a Mayfair drawing room, but it was still not the oddest part of the evening. After all, Lady Georgette Deveraux was no ordinary countess, despite her protestations on the matter.

For instance: there was a woman hanging upside down from her ceiling.

It was a very nice ceiling, painted with leaves enough to fill a jungle. There were filigree moldings, rococo accent, and pineapples. So many pineapples, all gold. The drapes were gold. The tables were gold. The mantelpiece was also gold and made the eyes water when a fire was lit. It was a lot to take in. Even at the best of times.

Aunt Georgie was not subtle.

She wasn't actually Summer's aunt—only Blackpool could rightfully claim Aunt Georgie. But she was so much more than that. Where Summer's mother was cold and critical and would not know fun if it bit her on her very perfect nose, Aunt Georgie was warm and kind and dramatic. Chaotic, to be truthful.

Summer loved her deeply. And she would avenge her in every way possible. Every day of the year. And with a great deal more alacrity than her irritating nephew.

"Hello, Maggie," Summer said to the woman attached to the

elaborate ceiling, before settling herself into a chair. She groaned. "This beard itches."

Maggie—acrobat, tightrope walker, and performance horse-woman—did not appear particularly sympathetic. She was upside down, so it was hard to tell. She still wore her costume from her recent performance, all spangles and beads. Her curly, dark hair was pinned ruthlessly, and her calves looked strong enough to kick a horse. She snorted at Summer's discomfort.

Definitely not sympathetic.

"Try wearing a leotard and grease paint," she said. "With one foot balanced on two different horses."

"I've worn three-foot ostrich feathers and paniers to meet the queen." Court fashions were ridiculous. "In a room that burned like the inside of hell and stank of a hundred different perfumes. And I did not gag."

Maggie rolled her eyes. Summer scratched harder.

"You'll mark your face," Aunt Georgie scolded her gently. Her silver curls were piled loosely on her head, and she wore pearls and a dressing gown with feathers on the hem to pour whiskey into teacups and offer frosted cakes to women planning criminal activities. Dramatic to the last. Her white skin was lined, soft brackets around her mouth and eyes. "You're too pretty to scar yourself, my dear."

"Never mind that," Beatrix said, joining them. She wore a simple brown dress, no jewelry, no frippery of any kind. She could have been anyone: a lady fallen upon genteel poverty, a maid, a vicar's daughter. Pale, freckled, and only pretending to be plain. "You'll give yourself away if you run about with a beard-shaped rash on your face."

Summer dropped her hand. She was useful because she was a duke's sister, and no one expected anything else from her. A beard-shaped rash, this week of all weeks, would draw unwanted attention. The attention she meant to draw was carefully curated. As carefully curated as the Sutherland art collection. *Former* Sutherland art collection.

Not former for very much longer.

Aunt Georgie glanced up at Maggie. "As we are all here, perhaps you might come down from there."

"But I'm comfortable."

"I have cakes."

"What kind?"

"Strawberry with lemon frosting."

Maggie dropped suddenly, catching herself with a strong flourish. Aunt Georgie winced. "Be careful, dear. I do hate it when you do that."

"But I'm so good at it." Maggie let herself drop the last few feet, before posing, as if waiting for applause. She settled for cake.

Beatrix eyed her, brow beetling. "Are you still using that same face paint?"

Maggie's cheeks were rouged, with exaggerated circles easy to see from the stands of the circus. The rest of her face was powdered to be pale, otherworldly. She shrugged. "It's fine."

"You know it contains lead! It will eat away at you and cause lesions. Use the rice powder."

"As soon as I find buried treasure under the circus ring to pay for it."

"I'll make some for you." There was no arguing with Beatrix when she knew something you did not.

Maggie stuffed a cake into her mouth.

"How was tonight?" Aunt Georgie asked.

"Itchy," Summer replied cheerfully.

Maggie wiped crumbs off her hands. "I used mostly flour and only a little gum Arabic for the paste," she said. "Don't pull at it. Use a bit of cooking oil and it should come away. Gin should work too." She grinned. "But I doubt Lady Sutherland has Blue Ruin on hand."

"I could send the butler to fetch some," Aunt Georgie said, unfazed. Mildly interested, even. "I've never had gin. Covent Garden?"

"Oil will be fine," Summer assured her. Aunt Georgie could

discover gin tomorrow.

"I'll fetch it," Beatrix said.

"I can go."

"Do you even know where it's kept?" she asked, not unkind-ly. "The kitchens are not small."

Summer wrinkled her nose, stopped when it pulled at the hair glued to her upper lip. "I suppose not."

Beatrix was quicker than was probably natural. She handed Summer a clay jug of olive oil and a cloth. Gratefully, Summer began to soak the beard from her skin.

"I've been hired as a kitchen maid for the event," Beatrix said, a bit smugly. "They don't have a housekeeper, and the butler is afraid of French delicacies. As is the cook, who only pretends to be from Paris. I mentioned *cerveau de veau* and *cassoulet* and they hired me on the spot."

"Lovely," Aunt Georgie said. She paused. "They are not actually serving calves' brain, are they?"

Maggie looked horrified. "That's revolting."

"No more so than steak and kidney pie," Beatrix pointed out.

"Bite your tongue. Steak and kidney pie is patriotic."

"It's mushy."

"I'm surprised they didn't accuse you of being a French spy," Summer said. The war touched London differently, she supposed. In Cornwall, every beach was watched with suspicion, every ship sighted a possible cause for alarm. The Thames wasn't likely to be overtaken by French warships.

"A Frenchie spy?" Beatrix blinked innocently. She did some-thing to her posture that made her practically invisible. She added a thick Covent Garden accent. "How's that likely, lovey? A girl like me, never out of the Garden. Don't even know where France is. But I've watercress, just picked today."

Summer grinned. She might be a lady, but even she knew not to eat the watercress. The water and soil in which it was grown was decidedly *not* clean. "One day an actual Garden girl is going to plant you a facer and she'll break your nose."

Beatrix just smirked.

"*Are* you a Garden girl?" Summer asked.

"I think she's Welsh," Aunt Georgie said. "I am sure I detected an accent."

As usual, Beatrix did not reply. "What did you discover?" she asked Summer instead, pencil and notebook at the ready. If she did not write it down, it had not happened.

"Three drawing rooms with pocket doors, which will be opened to create a main space. The conservatory will house the gala proper, the artwork and dancing, if there is to be any," Summer replied. "That's two skylights, two French doors to the gardens, three doors from the hallway, and six windows." She pulled the sketches out of her reticule. She'd thrown herself into the waiting hackney outside the club and immediately begun to draw.

Beatrix flipped through them, impressed. "These are good."

"They should be. That's twenty years of drawing masters at play. But there's more."

"Of course there is."

Summer glanced at Aunt Georgie. "Blackpool was there."

She sighed. "That boy."

"Did he see you?" Beatrix asked.

"Yes," Summer replied.

"Sloppy."

Summer glared, but only a little, since Beatrix was technically right.

"He recognized you?"

"Yes."

"In your very fine beard?" Aunt Georgie added.

"By the hairs on my chinny-chin-chin." He was never going to let her forget it, either. The man was intolerable.

"Hmm."

"What's that supposed to mean?" Summer demanded.

"Nothing, dear. I am old. We make noises."

Summer, Beatrix, and Maggie exchanged a glance so dry it

could have been used for kindling. Or French wine.

Summer suddenly very much wanted a glass of wine.

Aunt Georgie frowned. "Perhaps this was a silly idea after all." She wilted, just a little.

Summer would not have it. Aunt Georgie deserved her justice. And this little heist of theirs had made her smile for the first time in months. The loss of her husband of nearly fifty years had hit her very hard. If Summer had felt aimless, Aunt Georgie had been devastated.

"You are not suggesting we give up because of *Blackpool*," Summer said, thoroughly offended. "He cannot be allowed to win."

Maggie tilted her head. "Why not, exactly?"

"It's a law of nature. Like gravity. Blackpool does not win. I don't make the rules."

"I must have missed that class in school," Beatrix remarked drily.

"Besides, your nephew is not going to give you away," Summer added. "Well, not Blackpool, anyway."

Her other nephew was the new Earl of Sutherland, and he was rather self-occupied. Not to mention that if he could have married his title, he would have. It was everything to him. Hence why he was claiming this house within the day, as his due. Legally it was perfectly acceptable. Expected. But as it was the last place Aunt Georgie had lived with her husband before he died, Summer considered it an act of war. Damn primogeniture. Damn the entire British legal system.

"Eliot would not give you away either." Aunt Georgie nodded slowly. "That's true."

"He would absolutely give me away," Summer said. "Only I shan't let him."

"Hmm."

"What now?"

"Nothing, dear."

"We are so close now. And we are *not* giving up."

When Aunt Georgie's husband had died, he left his art to the Collectors, fearing that this nephew would sell his pieces and scatter them. But he did so on the understanding that the Mayfair Art Collectors Society would allow his wife to become a member. That she could visit the treasures they had bought on their travels together at her leisure, could see all the special pieces reserved for private viewings. It was not a common collection—nothing about Aunt Georgie was ordinary, so why would her tastes be any different? But she loved art. And secret societies. It was his last gift to her.

And then the Collectors reneged.

Not before accepting delivery of the art, of course. Little treasures, all. Memories of a life together. Summer remembered each of the pieces from her many visits. An odd little rooster, a mask that gave most people nightmares. A naughty drawing on a tile from Pompeii. She thought nothing of it. It was just part of their life.

And then the Collectors' founding members had the audacity to send Aunt Georgie a letter, signing all of their names. As if it wasn't something to be ashamed of. As if Summer hadn't memorized each and every signature.

"We're getting your collection back." She grabbed a golden pineapple mutinously, ignoring the edges that bit into her palm. "And we're keeping all of your pineapples."

Chapter Four

THE NEXT AFTERNOON, Summer went to the modiste. She took a turn about Hyde Park. She stopped at Gunter's for an ice. She went shopping for new evening gloves she did not need nor particularly want.

In short, she did all of the things Lady Summer would do. And she made certain that she was seen doing them.

All while avoiding Blackpool.

Honestly, the heist was the easier proposition. He seemed to have some preternatural sense as to where she would be next.

He was waiting for her outside the modiste, charming a circle of women aged nineteen to ninety, and two footmen who had that fascinated look in their eyes. It was a look she knew too well. It was constantly aimed at Blackpool's beautiful head. No wonder it was so big.

"Ladies, alas, I must not keep Lady Summer waiting."

There was a hum of disappointment. Summer hid a smile because it would only encourage him. "Lady Summer has no interest in your company right now," she said tartly. "I'm far too busy."

Someone gasped. Someone who did not know her, nor her friendship with Blackpool. If you could call it such. Did mildly fond antagonism and competition make for any kind of friendship? "You wound me, my lady," Blackpool returned, eyes gleaming.

"I might yet."

It was a game they knew all too well. And one she could not afford to play right now. Not with the gala looming and the questions she knew he was dying to ask her. She did not like lying to him. She had no problem at all with calling him out on his ridiculous flirting, his pretty face, every way in which he was wrong in his opinions on art and the way he played pall-mall, but lying felt different. It was something everyone else did, not them. Not to each other.

It was bothersome, but true.

Since she could not answer his questions and he would not change her mind nor she his, it was best to avoid him. They could recommence their skirmishes next week.

She was halfway down the block when Blackpool finally managed to pull away from his admirers. There was a lace handkerchief stuffed between the buttons of his coat. He blinked at it, looking younger, more genuine, than his usual smoldering. Lord, but the man could smolder.

For some reason, she preferred this expression.

"I never did understand these," he muttered.

"That is rather a lot of perfume." Summer wrinkled her nose. She could smell it over the horses and the dust kicked up by passing carriages. "Lilac, I think? And lemon?"

"Vile."

"Run along and return it, then."

"I think not. Who knows what I might come away with?"

"Three marriage proposals at least. Possibly a rash."

"Three? I must be losing my touch." They'd had a contest the spring of her coming out to see who could gather the most proposals, like roses for a posy. It had come to a tie.

She had managed to avoid him since the incident with the floorboards. She knew he had visited his great-aunt earlier this morning—she had hidden outside the door and eavesdropped on their conversation, which had resorted to near-begging on his part. He'd left even more frustrated than when he arrived. Aunt Georgie might look like dandelion fluff, but she was hard as a diamond through and through.

He was clearly very worried about the Collectors. More than was warranted at first glance. He knew something she did not.

And oh, how she hated that. She always had.

"Have you taken up pedestrianism?" Blackpool inquired, tipping his hat at a passing acquaintance. "Are we to race?"

She frowned at the change of subject. "What?"

"You are practically running. It's far too healthy for me. Although if I knocked over that old lady right there, I think I could beat you to the lamppost."

"That old lady is a patroness at Almack's and could take you down with just her hat."

"It is a rather fearsome hat. Is that meant to be a pigeon?"

She slid him a wry glance, refusing to acknowledge the question of whether she could beat him. She absolutely could, in a different dress. The skirts of the one she was wearing were far too narrow. "And since I'm trying to get away from you, you should sit right there on that bench and catch your breath, old man."

He nearly stumbled. "Old man?"

She tucked her tongue into her cheek, stifling a chuckle. "I do hear a distinct wheeze."

"I'm all of two years older than you!"

"I'm sure it's all in how you spend them," she said with false primness. "Wine and women do age a man."

He raised an eyebrow. "Are you calling into question my stamina?"

She swallowed. She actually had to swallow. It wasn't the silkiness of his voice—it was the dark promise, the dare that lay beneath it.

Before she could even begin to reply, an older woman threw herself in front of them, towing her very young and very embarrassed young lady behind her. "Lord Blackpool," she said, a touch too loudly. Passersby glanced in their direction.

"Lady Susan." Blackpool bowed. He was the very picture of civility, but Summer could read the tension in his shoulders. She almost felt sorry for him.

"I don't think you've met my goddaughter, Lady April Glass."

April curtsied, turning the exact shade of a raspberry ice.

"And April, this is Lady Summer. She is practically like a sister to the earl."

Blackpool recoiled. "Hardly."

"Oh, I beg your pardon."

Summer could not say why she liked his reaction so much, only that she did. He wasn't just smoldering—he was close to fuming.

"I hope you'll both join us for Lady April's coming-out ball," Lady Susan soldiered on, smothering any awkwardness with the sheer force of her will. April was ready to melt straight into the pavement. Lady Susan, a veteran of the Season, tightened her grip.

"Of course." Summer smiled at her gently. Her own mother had been an absolute nightmare the year she became a debutante, proposals notwithstanding. Actually, they fueled the nightmare when Summer had refused each and every one. "Have you made your curtsy to the queen, yet?"

Lady April gulped. "T-tomorrow."

"You'll be brilliant," Summer whispered conspiratorially. "It gets dreadfully hot at court, so have a peppermint before you go in. It will help with a nervous belly."

"And take note of Lady Summer's fashionable collar," Lady Susan said. "How clever, to starch the lace. It makes you look like a queen."

"Thank you,"

"Lady Summer was a diamond of the first water at her coming out. That was sixteen years ago, and they still call her the Diamond. Take note, dear."

"I could have done without the mathematics," Summer muttered.

She was thirty-three years old, and she had nothing to show for it except for a nickname given to her at the age of seventeen.

"Lady Summer has also had seventy-two marriage proposals. I do believe that is a record."

April's eyes widened. "Seventy-two?"

"One from a prince." Lady Susan sighed.

"It's not as impressive as it sounds," Summer said. "For one thing, that prince sent a proposal through the post. I have never even met him." More than half of those proposals had come from fortune hunters, and another good portion from those who wanted a duke for a brother-in-law. All of them considered her beautiful. But that was the game. That was Mayfair.

Her brother had saved her from the prince and suffered her mother's temper for a full two years. Summer was still suffering her disdain, but she considered it a fair trade.

"She's being modest," Blackpool said.

She had to smile. "I'm really not."

"I have a question, if you don't mind, Lord Blackpool," Lady Susan added, clearly desperate to keep his attention when he bowed again, preparing to walk on.

"Now's not the best time," Blackpool replied, with a reasonable approximation of regret. "I'm afraid Lady Summer and I have a previous engagement."

"Nonsense," Summer said cheerfully. "I'm in no hurry. I'll just pop into this shop here. I need a new feather for my bonnet."

"Is that so, pigeon?" He threw her a glance that practically dripped with distrust. She made her smile brighter in retaliation. Obnoxiously bright.

And then she slipped into the shop, marched down the aisle, and darted right out the back door.

THE WOMAN WAS trying to kill him.

He ought to be used to it by now.

Death by Lady Summer. By her mischievous grin, her unexpected comments, the curve of her waist. The smell of sweet oranges that clung to her.

He'd been dying at her hand since he was eighteen years old. To say he was accustomed to it was an understatement.

This was different. There had never been actual danger involved before now. The danger that she might dismember him with a lambchop at dinner was always present, but danger to himself he could account for. It meant nothing.

Danger to this infuriating woman meant everything.

He'd burn the Mayfair Art Collectors' precious house of treasures to the ground before letting them near her. The entire street. All of London.

He'd tried to talk Aunt Georgie into patience, into waiting just a little longer for the return of her collection. But without being able to offer her any concrete details, any reason at all beyond a sanctimonious plea for patience, he'd known it was a losing battle. He hadn't even attempted to ask Summer for patience. She had it in spades. But not for this.

And if she knew he had a secret, she would be merciless. Relentless. Awe inspiring.

Also at risk.

Unacceptable.

Dealing with the French, the English War Office, spies, and traitors was child's play compared to Summer. She was smarter than all of them combined, for one. She always, always saw more than she let on. The fact that she had secrets of her own was the only reason she had not immediately homed in on his. He planned to keep it that way for as long as possible.

The sooner he could get his hands on the list of spies, the location of the auction, the sooner she could break into any house she pleased in those breeches.

Those damned breeches.

He thought he'd fantasized about the shape of her backside before. It was nothing to knowing exactly how it flared out, how it might fit in his hand. He'd only had a glimpse as she ran away, when her coat flared out slightly. She'd actually thought that awful beard could fool him. As if he wouldn't know her from miles away. Blindfolded.

Someone should tell her that her disguise would have been more successful if she hadn't smelled so good. Like amber and oranges. Like Summer.

And now he was chasing her through London because he damn well knew she wouldn't let getting caught out stop her. Nothing stopped her.

She was about to kick over a hornet's nest, and like hell he would let them swarm over her.

Despite Lady Susan's insistent and terrifyingly strong grip on his arm. The woman must wrestle horses in her spare time, for all she looked like she was made of water. Her goddaughter was mortified, poor thing.

And Summer was smug and thrilled to her delectable toes.

She was always smug when ladies descended on him—a very different kind of hornet's nest. He'd kicked that one over when he was still a lad, and there was nothing for it now. But Summer never swarmed, never hovered.

She did sting. Frequently.

And he was perverse enough to enjoy it.

There was no use pretending he was not able to charm a lady at fifty paces. Mostly because he enjoyed it. He enjoyed them. Shy, sensual, bold, innocent. Wallflower. Widow. A wink, a smile, and they had an enjoyable evening between them.

A wink at Summer and she'd asked if he'd been bitten by a bug.

He'd laughed out loud. He hadn't been able to help himself. That was the first time he'd detected the faintest flush on her cheeks. The barest of wriggles as she sat with perfect posture in her chair.

He'd dreamt about it for weeks.

Her spicy-sweet scent faded as she disappeared into the shop. He ached to chase after her. Physically ached.

Lady Susan was still murmuring at him, her grip like winter

ice. Carriages trundled past, ladies walked with footmen hurrying after them, men tipped their hats, streetsweepers wielded their brooms for pennies. Someone laughed.

This was Summer's world.

He wouldn't let anyone take it away from her.

HE FOUND HER in Hyde Park.

Of course he did.

Summer might have been disappointed if he hadn't. They had a pattern, after all. An unspoken agreement. Quiet battles waged over canapes and champagne, pearls and parasols. Sometimes, very late at night, over the billiards table. Nothing scandalous. The door was always left open. But they competed fiercely, quips and jests flying between them.

Those were her favorite nights.

Once again, what that said about her current nights was mildly depressing.

Only she didn't feel depressed. She felt invigorated. Partly due to her secret plans, partly due to knowing Blackpool was out there. Searching for her. She could run circles around most people of her acquaintance. They saw what they wanted to see. Not Blackpool.

She loved it.

Even when she hated it.

She kept her smile easy, her stride steady. Just another walk through Hyde Park to see and be seen. Mostly to be seen. A diamond must glitter, after all. Nothing about her usual schedule could differ. Not that she expected anyone to suspect her. Why would they? Ladies did not steal from art societies. They did not steal from powerful men. They did not steal at all. Duke's sisters did not glue fake beards to their faces.

They did not ask questions, or care for answers.

Still. She liked to do things right. Especially something like this. It meant everything to Aunt Georgie. She would not be caught out by Blackpool. Not again.

She nodded greetings as she walked, accepted bows and tips of the hat. She gave her opinion on a new bonnet, the idea of an escritoire painted with lilies.

The *ton* wandered on foot and passed by in elaborate carriages cleaned and polished to a shine. It smelled of sunshine and horses and perfume. Birds hid in the trees, affronted, no doubt, by the sheer volume of feathers pinned to bonnets and cuffs. The new trend was a bit disconcerting, until you got used to it. Giant ostrich feathers balanced on the head to make your curtsy to the queen was bad enough, and now it was pigeon feathers dyed pink, green duck feathers, glossy crow feathers bristling from necklines and dress hems and cuffs. Even the very elegant, crowned gentlemen's hats were not immune.

And she was just another bird. *Flutter, flutter.*

Was that Blackpool over there by the Serpentine, feeding the ducks? A closer look. No. Not him.

Anticipation fizzed inside her.

She wanted to tell herself it was strictly due to the clandestine events. But she knew herself too well sometimes. Too much of this anticipation was tangled up in wondering if Blackpool was watching her right now. It tingled through her, right down to her thighs.

Another reason to rout him thoroughly.

He had no business affecting her this way. She knew his tricks too well.

And yet...

She had to tamp down a ridiculous trickle of disappointment when she found herself back at her waiting carriage. Blackpool had not followed her. He had not found her.

Truly, why would he? The games they played were in the moment. They did not require sustained effort. Despite the urgency in his reaction to finding her in the Collectors' house, to his pleas with his great-aunt.

Enough now. Back to work. Focus.

"Lady Summer." His voice was like melted chocolate, damn

the man. And he absolutely knew it. She heard the smirk and the smugness lacing every word. It ought to have put her off.

It made her thighs clench instead.

Inconvenient, that.

And secretly delightful. She would never let him know he affected her, of course. She wouldn't be one of his many honeybees, hovering at the hive.

She paused, glancing up slowly, as if bored. "Took you long enough, Blackpool."

He grinned. He was perched on the driving bench next to her coachman. Very proper, even in its impropriety. A hundred pairs of eyes watched them even now. The charming rakehell and the Diamond. It would be in the gossip paper by morning. There would be sketches.

"I'm gratified to hear you were eager for my arrival."

She narrowed her eyes. "Not quite."

"Admit it, you missed me."

"Like I'd miss a poke in the eye with a sharp stick."

"You'll hurt my feelings."

"The care and feeding of your enormous ego is not one of the things that keeps me up at night."

His surprised laugh cracked out. Then his voice lowered. "What does keep you up at night, plum?"

She was embarrassed to admit she had to swallow before answering. She'd been called many things—Venus, Rose, Diamond—but "plum" made her feel like blushing for no particular reason. "How best to drown you in the Serpentine, of course."

"Of course." He knew she was lying. It was there in his face, in his dark eyes, the quirk of his lips.

"What are you doing up there?" She hid herself behind the expected scowl.

"Waiting for you."

"Well, here I am."

"Here you are." Again, the soft words, something stronger

underneath. A promise. A challenge.

She so hated to turn down a challenge.

"I'm here to escort you home," he said.

"I don't recall asking you to."

"We need to talk." Softer still, for her ears only.

He wanted answers. He would read her like a book if she let him. "No, thank you."

"That wasn't a request."

Goodness. That tone again. The answering hot tug in her center.

"Go away, Blackpool."

"Get in the carriage, Summer."

"It's *my* carriage. My coachman." She glared at him pointedly. He had the grace to redden. But what coachman would refuse an earl? And this earl in particular?

"People are staring, plum."

She huffed out an impatient sigh. Let them stare, just for a moment. Whatever rumors resulted from it would be tiresome, but ultimately helpful, because they had nothing to do with art and theft.

Finally, she stepped up into her carriage, settling on the emerald-green velvet seats. The windows were open to the spring breeze, to Blackpool's order. "Drive on."

He thought he'd won this round.

He would think it all the way through the London streets, right to the red door of her house in Mayfair. Until he peered into the carriage and found it empty.

She snuck out when they stopped for a snarl of traffic. She ducked into the crowd on the sidewalk and ran to Aunt Georgie's house, grinning the entire way.

Chapter Five

THE MAYFAIR ART Collectors Society, rot them, knew how to host a party.

It galled Summer to admit it.

It was already the event of the Season, and this was just a preview. Merely a teaser, a private exclusive showing meant to whet the appetite. The rest of London would clamor to buy tickets once they saw the aristocracy was also interested. It was the Collectors' working theory, at any rate.

The street outside was clogged with carriages as members of the *ton* flooded toward the entrance in their silk dresses and starched cravats, jewels gleaming, hair curled just so. Summer had dressed very carefully in silk and emeralds, but more importantly, under her gown her embroidered stockings had leather garters strong enough to hold a dagger, a lockpick, and loops on which to attach pilfered goods.

She was more excited than she had been to make her curtsy to the queen all those years ago.

This was serious work, she reminded herself.

But it was also *fun*.

Lamps gleamed at the window and from the edge of the steps leading her to the front door, opened to the influx of chattering guests. There was nothing Mayfair loved more than the hint of novelty. But they would be bored again by morning. She knew the cycle all too well.

And the pontification was exactly as expected. Arrogant. Eye-rolling. Occasionally correct.

Summer eavesdropped on several more conversations as she made her way through toward the gallery, stopping to greet people, to comment on the Greek vase with the carved minotaur, which she coveted. On a Rembrandt and a Caravaggio. She would take a turn about the ballroom just to be remembered there, in the thick of the public space, no interest or thought to anything but dancing and admiring rare artwork.

Ha.

Her behavior would not be obviously linked to this house, or this party, or *that* painting which was about to go missing. Not that they would notice for quite some time, if all went to plan.

She tried not to grin.

"Why must you insist on wearing that common color?"

Worse than old men stealing art that was not theirs to steal?

Her mother.

Why was her mother *here*, of all places?

Summer took a deep breath and turned around. "Mother."

The Dowager Duchess Tremaine was dressed in silvery gray, dripping with pearls, as was her custom. The tiara tucked into her hair had diamonds set round a gray pearl the size of a quail's egg. Summer wondered, once again, if her mother was so peevish because her neck ached from carrying around so many jewels. She'd asked her once and been smacked with her fan for her trouble. Summer had taken it as a yes.

"What are you doing here?"

Her mother sniffed. "Everyone is here. Don't slouch."

"I'm not slouching, Mother."

"You're in great danger of falling out of that dress altogether. It's indecorous."

"It's perfectly fashionable." And only a tiny, teeny bit inde-cent. A suggestion of inappropriateness. And as usual, spending more than a few minutes in her mother's presence made a headache pulse behind her right eye. She'd spent so many years craving that attention. Now she only wanted to be rid of it.

"Where have you been?" her friend Ophelia interrupted before Summer could say something inflammatory.

Summer gave very serious consideration to kissing Lady Ophelia right then and there. Possibly proposing marriage.

"Oh, Lady Tremaine," Ophelia added. "I beg your pardon. I did not see you there."

The dowager duchess peered at Ophelia through her quizzing glass. "Lady Kennet."

Ophelia dropped a very respectful curtsy worthy of the royal court. "That tiara is stunning, Your Grace."

"Thank you. You always did have lovely manners. See what you can do about my daughter, would you?"

"I shall endeavor to try."

They waited until Summer's mother had stalked away before Summer snorted. "Lovely manners, my arse. You once rode bareback in men's breeches through London."

"Just the once. And your mother doesn't know that." Ophelia hugged her, looking like someone out of a fairy story with her pale hair and pink diaphanous gown sewn with spangles. Her eyes were moonlight pale and uncanny. Summer adored her. "Anyway, where have you been? It's been dull as dishwater without you."

"I've missed you too. I was in the country with Tessa." As Tessa had a trick chandelier rigged up to knock any unwanted guests unconscious, it had been a very educational visit.

"That was ages ago."

"I suppose it was." It had made her question her own life, her own privileges. And then Aunt Georgie's husband had died and there were more pressing matters. "Also, I was avoiding my mother."

"That is rather taxing. Next time, avoid her in my drawing room, if you please."

"Agreed."

Beatrix moved through the crowd beside them, murmuring to the butler, the footmen. She did not glance in Summer's direction even once, which was how Summer knew her presence had been noted. She did nod, barely, which was also how Summer knew the painting she was after was right where it was supposed to be. Aunt Georgie had stayed at home, much as she longed to rub the collective noses of the Collectors in her imminent and ever-so-slightly-criminal triumph. Maggie was probably perched on the rooftop even now, waiting.

"Lady Summer, you are as bright as the summer sun," Lord Fernsby said, bowing over her hand.

"Thank you," she replied. *Seventeen,* she thought. That was the seventeenth time this Season alone that she was compared to the summer sun.

"Not just the sun," Lord Southwark broke in. "But the entire summer."

Three more gentlemen and two ladies turned to bring her into the conversation, to garner her opinion on the portrait of Lord Fernsby by Sir Joshua Reynolds. Two more viscountesses joined, their lady's maids having sewn late into the night to add starched lace to their collars, duplicating her walking dress from the day before.

The talk turned to the war, as it always did.

"It will be over in weeks," Lord Southwark scoffed. "No one can beat the Royal Navy. We own the Channel."

Lord Fernsby inclined his head in Summer's direction. "We ought to keep the conversation pleasant for the ladies. A Diamond like Lady Summer is not interested in such talk."

Lady Summer knew perfectly well that the Raid on Boulogne had not been materially successful, mostly due to the failure of new equipment designed by the inventor Robert Fulton. Although only one French ship had ended in flames, and it had still reminded Bonaparte that the British were kings of the sea. Which was a timely reminder, as Spain had recently declared its intent on joining France.

All remarks that would have shocked the guests to hear Summer speak aloud. As if she did not read the newspapers. As if she was not from Cornwall, where the war touched quicker and rougher.

Once again, she swallowed her comments and smiled.

THE GUESTS HAD been gathered long enough that the inebriation was starting to show.

Perfect.

This was her moment.

Her window of time was brief. There were too many footmen dashing back and forth with trays and cloaks and housemaids sewing up fallen hems, couples seeking privacy, wallflowers seeking an escape. And too many of those footmen seemed unnaturally large and without any experience carrying trays balanced with crystal glasses. Curious.

Summer darted up the main staircase, ducking into the third parlor on the left. It stank of cheroot smoke. The landscape painting was banished from the main gallery on the grounds that it was too small and dark to be properly seen.

To say Aunt Georgie was infuriated was an understatement. She had bought it for her husband on their honeymoon in Italy. It was not Summer's favorite, but she was far too smart to say so. She certainly would not have bothered to steal it because she *liked* it. But it was very old, very cherished, and, best of all, waiting for her right where it was supposed to be.

There was a spill of light from the lamps and torches burning outside, just enough to see by. The moon snuck in through the windows to peek at the gold thread embroidery of a wall hanging, the rococo embellishments curving over the doorways, the silver and pearl buttons on her gloves. Noted. Next time, no silver, no pearls. It caught the light too easily.

With a last glance toward the door, she took down the painting and crouched behind a tall settee overrun with plump cushions. She liberated the canvas from the frame with a few strokes of her knife, and then untucked the forgery from one of her garters. She unrolled it, slid it into the frame, and secured it with a twist of putty and a few taps. She would have liked more time to adjust it with proper nails or even a bit of glue. But that wasn't the objective. Perfection would not serve her tonight. Only haste.

Oh, it chafed. She could do so much better. So much more.

Maggie was going to drop through the skylight. Beatrix had already pocketed a Leonardo da Vinci sketch and a bear carved from amber, all while running a staff of thirty.

Summer had painted a picture. A good one, to be sure. But you couldn't throw a stone in Mayfair without hitting a lady who *painted*.

Never mind that now. Time enough for an existential crisis over a cup of tea in the morning. Tonight was about triumph. Revenge. Justice.

She rolled the original artwork tightly and tucked it into her garter. Her dress billowed down, hiding all evidence. The frame went back up on its hook over the mantelpiece. Who hung expensive antique artwork over a smoky fireplace? Honestly, it *deserved* to be stolen.

She observed the handiwork. Nothing disturbed, no bits of frayed canvas left behind, and nothing to suggest someone had poked about.

She had prepared for this as well as she had prepared for her foray into the house while wearing a beard. This time, if she was caught: she was turned around looking for the ladies' retiring room, had a headache, or needed a moment of quiet. No one was likely to question her.

If the frame would not release its painting: the whole lot would have gone out the window and been retrieved from the back garden. Hopefully before it rained. Or else tucked under the settee for Beatrix to collect later.

If she was caught red-handed: she had noticed the painting was crooked on its hook and was merely fixing it. Less likely, as she had locked the door behind her.

No one had any reason to suspect her, in any case.

Except for Lord Blackpool. Again.

And now here he was, exactly where he should not be.

And he knew it, smirking at her from across from the doorway like the handsome bastard he was. Leaning against the wall, in his fine evening clothes, waistcoat the color of plums. Why must he always lean on things? Was it because he was so tall? He probably thought it took away from his aura of leashed power, made him look harmless somehow. Languid.

Ha.

It only made her wonder what would stir him to move toward her.

"Are you lurking again, Blackpool?" she asked, covering an instinctive need to glance behind her, to fiddle, to give herself away. To fix her hair. There was no way in hell she would give herself away as one more person who wondered if he'd noticed her. If he thought about her at all when they weren't busy bothering each other to distraction.

"Or is it simply too tiring to hold up that swelled head of yours and you must prop yourself up in dark corners for a rest?" she added.

There. That was better. More natural. For them, anyway.

He pushed away from the wall, still smirking. But his eyes narrowed on her. "I told you it wasn't safe here. What are you up to now?"

"Nothing." The rolled-up canvas of a painting worth an obscene number of pounds scratched the inside of her thigh.

It was clear he didn't believe her. But he couldn't prove that she was lying. That put a jaunt in her step. Her plans would hold up.

"Summer."

The way he said her name… It ought to be illegal.

Because she could not afford to notice the way it tingled through her, the way it uncoiled heat inside her body, she lifted her chin. "Blackpool."

"You are definitely up to something."

She rolled her eyes. "You always think that."

"And I'm aways right."

She snorted. No one else could make her roll her eyes and snort like a pig at market. She was known for her elegance, her sophistication. Bloody sonnets had been written about her. Bad ones. But the point remained: no snorting mentioned.

"Are you meeting someone?" he asked sharply, traces of their usual teasing and needling suddenly vanishing.

She did not pretend to misunderstand. Abandoned drawing rooms and dark hallways were made for lovers. And as she was far from a debutante with need of a chaperone, her options were far more plentiful. Still, some care was required. A reputation was only helpful when it served you. Her mother maintained that a certain duty was required to the ducal family name. Summer had always thought if she was afforded such privilege, why waste it? Was she meant to wither away for lack of wanting a husband? Pretend she did not inhabit a body that had needs?

Probably.

She did not do well with being told what to do. Consequences did not often find her. She was a woman of a certain age with a certain understanding of the world; she knew how to comport herself. How to handle her business. How to keep a secret.

Not that she had had any secrets to keep lately. Certainly nothing juicy. *More's the pity.*

And never with Blackpool.

Not since that kiss when she was seventeen. Not her first, but certainly the only one she remembered so well. Too well. Not that it mattered. It hadn't mattered to him then, and it didn't now. She was one of a thousand kisses. They preferred aggravating each other.

It was a far less enjoyable way to heat the blood. Still, better than nothing.

She enjoyed their skirmishes. Even when she wanted to

throw things at his head. Heavy things. And since his reputation was far worse than hers, she certainly did not owe him any explanations. Ordinarily, she would have told him exactly that. With much stronger wording. Possibly also with that heavy object tossed at his fat head.

But tonight, she needed to throw him off the scent. He already knew what they were about. Finding her here wearing a beard, his fruitless conversation with his Aunt Georgie—much as she liked to call him an idiot, he was not. And they had already dismissed him from his job of retrieving the collection. He knew it all.

He just wanted her to admit to it. He wanted the details. In order to stop them, for whatever reason.

Not on her watch.

She twisted her finger through the heavy curl that lay across her collarbone. His dark eyes followed the movement, flared, damped down to smoldering ember. Interesting. She let her fingertip trail over her bare skin.

"Summer." He all but growled her name.

Oh, this *was* a fun game. It was so very tempting to see who would break first.

But alas.

"What if I am?" she asked archly, refusing to wonder why she both wanted to poke at any possible jealousy, and also assure him she was not attached. *Head in the game, my girl.* "What if I *am* meeting someone?"

"Are you?" He stepped closer.

She shrugged one shoulder idly, just this side of disdainfully. She liked to see how far she could push him. She never understood why, but there it was. "That's not your concern, is it?"

"Who is it?" He glared over her head into the dark drawing room. "Is he in there, hiding behind the settee? Very brave."

"Hardly. I'm going back to the ballroom. Are you coming?"

"No."

"Suit yourself." She smiled, showing all of her teeth. Not at all genteelly. A warning, not an enticement. "Again, I'll remind you, not your business."

He pushed past her, into the drawing room.

She didn't stop to think—she never did when he was involved. Annoyance, a competitive streak, and something else she would not name; it all fired her into wanting to best him. Before he bested her.

The threat was always there. Sometimes it sent the most inappropriate thrill through her.

"No," he said darkly. "It's not a man, not here and not tonight. And the art downstairs is too big to cart away without being seen."

If he only knew.

He stepped closer. The fact that he could read her better than anyone never failed to rankle. Excite. Intrigue. "Tell me," he added, a clear command, and so unlike the Blackpool she knew that she merely blinked up at him for a moment.

Someone else answered for her.

"I'm telling you, one of the bells was cut. The alarms can't be trusted now. Check everything."

She stared at Blackpool. He stared back. There was no pretending they hadn't wandered away from the party, into forbidden areas, that there wasn't more going on that they were willing to admit to. That they weren't circling each other.

Even though the men couldn't know about the canvas rolled under her skirts, they'd know *her*. The invitation list was vetted, and long sought after. As a duke's twin sister, she did not often blend in, even when she thought she might want to. Which, admittedly, was not very often.

Blackpool cursed, and then he was backing her into a shadowy corner. The framed forgery hung innocently over the fireplace. She tried not to glance at it. Beatrix reminded her daily that it was a dead giveaway when someone was trying to hide something. Not that it mattered—this corner would not hide them either. There wasn't even a potted plant to shield them.

"Blackp—"

"Not a word," he said, before his mouth closed over hers.

She was being kissed by Eliot Howard, Earl of Blackpool.

Thoroughly.

Sinfully.

Was this even kissing? Surely, there had to be another word for this. It was a claiming, a desperate need. He sucked on her lower lip before teasing her tongue with his, before taking her mouth like he had been dreaming about it for years. Like he might die without another taste.

"Don't move," he commanded. "Don't you dare move."

He pushed against her, his hardness pressing into her heat so forcefully that she moaned.

She actually moaned. Out loud.

"That's it," he said against her mouth. "That's the sound."

Her quim went instantly hot, feeling full, swollen. Her nipples pebbled under her dress. She gasped when his lips closed on her throat and sucked, hard. She felt it everywhere. His hand gripped her knee, lifting her leg, opening her more fully to the onslaught of his body. He was hard, muscled, hungry. For *her*.

And confused.

He paused.

Right. He wasn't just pressing against her—he was also pressing against a painting, a dagger, several tools of criminal activity. "Goddamn it, Summer."

She grinned at him because she didn't know what else to do.

Actually, she knew exactly what she *wanted* to do.

She wanted to grind and squirm against him until it was the only thing he could think about. She wanted it badly enough that she fought the inclination.

His eyes narrowed on her mouth. "No pretending," he said darkly. "Not anymore."

He kissed her again, or she kissed him. They collided, and she wouldn't have been surprised if sparks had shot in the air. She wondered that the walls did not catch fire. The entire bloody townhouse. She clutched at his arms, just because she could. The firm muscles moved under her palms as he held her more securely, tangled his fingers in her hair and tightened until she moaned again. She was trapped between him and the wall, and she loved it. She *loved* it. He licked into her mouth, the rhythm unspooling something inside of her. Something delicious. Something new.

She nearly forgot where she was.

"This parlor is off-limits," someone barked from behind them.

It took an embarrassingly long moment for Summer to remember that the bark was directed at them. Her body was heavy with desire, pinned to the wall by Blackpool. Blackpool, who never wasted a moment when it could be used to tease her or dare her to do something ridiculous. He had never taken her seriously. So it was some consolation that when he finally pulled back, his eyes were as wild as she felt. He was not unaffected. She was not alone in feeling like she was about to melt away. Like the moment could not be taken back. Could not be forgotten.

He still had her pinned to the wall. She wasn't entirely sure her legs could hold her. After one kiss. Ridiculous. But also true.

He turned his head slightly. "Bit busy here."

The other man snorted. "Aye."

Blackpool tensed. He tucked her more deeply into the corner but kept her leg clamped to his hip. He was hiding her with his body. They would see a ruffle of skirts. "Sod off, mate."

"You can't be in here," the guard insisted.

Blackpool was trying to protect her reputation. It was sweet. And necessary, but not for the reason he was thinking. If a guard noticed her now, he would notice her all night. She'd never get the rest of her tasks completed. She'd be useless.

She must have stiffened at the thought, because Blackpool's gaze found hers. She tried for a nonchalant smile. He scowled. For some reason, that made her smile more, despite their predicament. "Happy to leave," Blackpool told the guard, his eyes never leaving hers. "But not until you sod off. The lady's not for gawking at."

The guard snorted again. "Lady. Right."

Blackpool turned, very slowly, still keeping her shielded. "Pardon?"

Whatever he saw in Blackpool's face made the guard swallow, despite being twice his size and bulk. "Meant nothing by it."

"I'm thrilled to hear it," Blackpool replied, tone somehow both mild and cutting. "You'll turn your back. I'm a member here, but if that's not enough, you'll tell anyone who asks that it was the Earl of Blackpool you found in the parlor. If they have questions, they can find me."

Bollocks. When they found the forgery, they would blame him.

A problem for later, she reminded herself.

The guard turned around. Blackpool ushered Summer into the hall, still blocking her with his body in case the man should turn around for a peek. The candles flickered in the sconces. Someone was playing a pianoforte downstairs. Conversations thrummed, like the roar of the ocean. "Go," Blackpool murmured. "I'll find you."

"No need," she said lightly.

It was just a kiss, and she had work to do.

His hand tightened briefly on her hip. "I'll find you."

SUMMER LOST HERSELF in the chattering crowd, wondering why Blackpool's kiss suddenly felt like the most dangerous part of the evening.

And the most delicious.

Damn him. Again.

She wandered, finding herself by a shelf of vases. They were displayed proudly, but not hidden under a protective bell jar like some of the others. It did not belong to Aunt Georgie. The name on the card attached: Lord Glass.

One of the members who had stolen Aunt Georgie's collection, and then attempted to sell one of the paintings even though they did not belong to him, but to the society.

And here was his precious fish vase.

It was Greek in origin, at least two thousand years old, red and black and reasonably small. Flowers ran along the opening, with a repeating labyrinth pattern along the bottom. Between them was painted a man with a surprisingly full head of air, and wings.

Riding a very large fish.

Was that a fish? A dolphin, perhaps? She'd never seen a dolphin, but, she hazarded, nor had the artist. All she knew for certain was that it fit quite nicely into her pocket. She'd sewn it herself, three times the size of a regular pocket, and never mind that ball gowns covered in lace and embroidery did not generally offer pockets. The vase slid down and bumped lightly against her knee. It pulled slightly at the lines of her dress, but not enough to draw any serious attention. Especially by candlelight and several gallons of wine.

There was no reason for her to steal it.

Except that she wanted to.

Something about this whole night was pricking at her, reminding her that she could be so much more, with just a little effort. Her friend Tessa took in women on the run from violent men, heiresses in grave danger, ladies who found themselves friendless.

Summer took in her hem when the fashions changed.

That wasn't precisely true. She loved her life and her place in Society. She was not so naïve as to be ungrateful for her privileges. Not at her age, not knowing how different her life would be without a brother's coronet to shield her. But knowing what Tessa did and helping her as best she could this past autumn had awakened something inside her. Watching Maggie defy gravity and Beatrix defy every expectation in a way that somehow also left her invisible had made Summer even keener to prove herself. If only to her own self with none the wiser. She could never be invisible. She could dance an exquisite cotillion, paint like a

French master, speak Italian, plan a dinner for thirty couples.

And she could steal back what was unrightfully stolen.

And here was a man riding a fish.

Fate, surely.

She just wanted to prove to herself that she had a few talents of her own. Something unexpected. And it occurred to her that it would be better if the only art missing at the end of the evening did not belong to Aunt Georgie. Hardly subtle.

Tempting. It was so very tempting to rub their noses in it.

But then they would have to deal with retaliation, possibly a Bow Street Runner. Most definitely a small parade of affronted gentlemen with wounded egos, sniffing and scolding and lecturing.

Honestly, it sounded exhausting.

She preferred a man riding a fish.

BLACKPOOL FOUND HER, as promised.

She was not surprised this time.

She was already accepting her cloak from a footman who had no idea where the cloaks were kept and had disappeared for a quarter of an hour. Blackpool grabbed it from him and assisted her himself. "You're going home." He was rarely so demanding. Usually, every word dripped with soft charm, with promise. Not tonight.

He proceeded to escort her down the front walk toward the carriages and the waiting horses. *Escort* was perhaps not the right word. *Propel* was more accurate. "I most certainly am not going home." And only partly because he'd told her to do just that.

"Well, you're not staying here."

She dug in her heels a little. It was the principle of the thing.

"Summer, I will put you over my shoulder."

The threat should not have simmered between them.

Too late.

The heat of it flushed her cheeks. She knew exactly how he kissed now that he was a man grown. What a nuisance that he was so very good at it.

"Get in the carriage," he said through his teeth.

As she could not afford to waste any more time arguing—as much as she might like to—she opted for a change of strategy. Even though she always liked it when the muscle in his jaw twitched like that. She wanted to bite it.

That was new.

Blame it on the stolen kiss, the general excitement of the evening. Nothing more.

Back to strategy.

She smiled meekly. "Yes, my lord."

He froze, then groaned like a man out to sea. "That sends a bolt of pure terror through me, I don't mind telling you."

"What does?" she asked innocently.

"Any hint of compliance coming from you."

"I'm sure I don't know what you mean." She flashed him a smile over her shoulder, couldn't help it. She tried not to waddle. Between the rolled-up canvas and the vase, she felt a bit like a market basket with legs. "But you *have* been paying attention. I suppose I should be flattered."

"To you?" he asked, shutting the door firmly behind her. "Always"

Chapter Six

"W AS THAT MY nephew?" Aunt Georgie inquired.
Summer yelped. Only a little. But still, it wasn't
very stealthy of her. She rubbed the spot over her heart, which
had somersaulted in her chest. "What are you doing here?"

Aunt Georgie sniffed. "It's my collection—why shouldn't I be
here?"

"Because it's hardly subtle," Summer suggested drily, dropping onto the seat opposite her.

"Nonsense. I'll stay right here in the carriage." Aunt Georgie
wore a black dress, no doubt left over from her mourning period.
A jaunty veil of black lace sprouted from her bonnet. "I'm very
inconspicuous. Like a shadow."

If shadows also wore gold pineapple earrings and bright yellow laces through their slippers.

Aunt Georgie followed Summer's gaze. "One must have
some joy."

"I completely agree." Aunt Georgie had been saying those
very words to her since she was a child falling in and out of
scrapes. Especially when she was caught by her mother.

Aunt Georgie was not fond of the Dowager Duchess of Tremaine. And not just because Summer's mother abhorred
pineapples.

Summer hiked her gown up to knees, something else her

mother would have abhorred. Aunt Georgie did not even blink. Summer untucked the painting from her garter. Her thigh was red and scratched. She unrolled the canvas with a flourish. "Voila!"

Aunt Georgie's eyes sheened with tears almost immediately. "Oh, there she is," she murmured. "Harold bought that in Florence from an estate sale. A local count with failing vineyards and a card-counting habit."

"Wouldn't that imply he was good at gambling?"

"Perhaps he would have been if he'd been better at card counting." She ran a knobby finger over the brushstrokes. "Practice, Summer." Another declaration she had made since Summer was very young. Pianoforte? Practice. Horseback riding? Practice? Throwing peas at her brother when he was being pompous? Practice. One mustn't waste peas.

"I know, Aunt Georgie. And should I decide to take up card counting, I promise I shall practice most diligently."

Aunt Georgie nodded distractedly, still staring at the painting of green hills under a gray sky, caught in her memories. When her mouth began to tremble, Summer pulled out the vase and plopped it down on the cushion beside her.

Aunt Georgie blinked at the fish-man with his wings. "That's not one of my mine."

"I know. But I rather like him."

"It's hideous."

"Yes."

"I love it."

"I thought you might." Summer grinned. "It belongs to Lord Glass. Well, *belonged*."

"I'm keeping it. It seems only fair, as he has kept most of my collection."

"Exactly so."

"I might even display it at my next soiree. Three fish courses, a swan in a cream sauce. Red and black dresses, the footmen in togas. Lord Glass will turn positively puce."

"I'll be sure to tell him there are dreadful forgeries of this very vase floating around London."

They exchanged a grin. "He'll have an apoplectic fit on my drawing room floor."

"One Collector down..."

SUMMER COULD ADMIT to a twinge of jealousy as she watched Maggie flatten herself to the roof of the conservatory. To know exactly what your body was capable of, to trust yourself enough to fly in the face of gravity. It must have felt a little like flying.

The problem with flying, aside from the inevitable plummet, was that the sky was already full: of stars, or smoke, or birds. All things people had a tendency to crane their necks back to watch, to point out to others. Even at three o'clock in the morning, as the gallery doors were being locked to guests, and they trickled home. The street slowly cleared, the sounds of horses' hooves ringing all around. It was smog and shadows and damp and spangles come loose from silk gowns.

They were nearly done.

Nearly.

One painting left to steal tonight, hung up so high that the frame touched the ceiling cornices. Never mind the locked doors—the trick floorboards were their most pressing problem. It was too quiet now to cover their creaking and the painting too high for a quick grab.

But not for Maggie.

She didn't need a floor. She had the roof, the skylight, ropes, and a complete disregard for broken bones.

She did, however, also need a spot of privacy.

Which would not have been a problem, if it weren't for three guests, distracted on their way to their carriage by the streaks of pink lightning in the clouds above. It was beautiful, eerie.

And it was a complete pain in the arse. More than Blackpool, and that was saying something.

Summer pushed the hood of her cloak back and removed one

of her earrings, a ruby drop surrounded by tiny seed pearls. She had bought them when she was nineteen, the very day her mother had scolded her for wearing red, a color too racy for a debutante. She'd bought a basket of red ribbons the same day, as well as red silk roses for her bonnets and crimson silk slippers that had made her mother sputter with outrage. Her entire focus was usually on her brother Callum, the poor sod, but back then Summer had still wanted her mother's attention. Needling her for scoldings and shocked gasps had seemed worth it.

She tucked the earbob into the top of her evening glove and hurried along the flagstone path to the patch of garden at the side where the two women and the one gentleman were murmuring excitedly over the lightning. Her skin prickled in the sudden drop in temperature, from unseasonably warm to the more usual London damp.

Maggie clung to the roof, busy hanging as much of her body through the skylight as she could. When she finally retrieved the painting, the garden had to be empty. And not just because Summer would throw herself bodily on such a work of art to protect it from the rain.

Summer smiled, like a duke's sister and not like a woman committing crime and very much enjoying it. "Sir Lucas, is that you?"

He turned around, nearly lost his balance, recovered admirably. "Lady Summer." He bowed, teetered, but only slightly. She didn't know the two ladies but sent them a friendly and conspiratorial smile.

"I'm so glad you're here," she said. "I think I lost my earring earlier when I was admiring the hyacinths." She motioned to her naked lobe and then to the ruby drop in the other ear. "Could I trouble you to help me find it? The footmen seem rather fearsome."

"They do, don't they?" the lady with red hair murmured. "I saw one as big as a house." She winked. "I like it, but his scowl made my sister cry."

"Your sister cries when the wind blows the curtains too hard," her friend muttered.

"True. Still."

She wasn't wrong. Summer knew footmen, and the Collectors had an odd lot. They were protecting the art of several earls and viscounts and even a duke, but there was still something a little dodgy about some of them. She half expected shady debts to be collected right here in the converted ballroom.

"My brother gave me these earrings for our birthday," she added, bringing them back to the point of her approach. Also, it never hurt to bring up a duke. Callum had been more useful when he was single, but as she thoroughly enjoyed her sister-in-law, Summer would let it pass. "He'll never let me forget it if I lose them."

"Of course we'll help," Sir Lucas assured her. He'd already lost his hat.

"Brothers are beastly," the redhead commiserated.

And then they all lowered their heads and helped her scour the ground, helpfully turning their attention away from the lightning and the rooftop and Maggie. They inspected potted hyacinths, sifted through the grass growing between the flagstones, picked through the roots of a lilac. She gave Maggie as long as she could, but when the first raindrop hit her backside, Summer dropped her earring from her gloves into a bit of moss growing between two stones. She jostled Sir Lucas until he finally noticed it, blinking blurrily. Another raindrop hit her hip.

"Found it!" he finally cried, grabbing for it like it might turn into a sparrow and fly away.

"Thank you so much," Summer said, accepting it with a grateful smile. "You're all very kind."

The wind changed direction. More rain spattered.

"I'll let you go before you get drenched," she added, shooing them into the street before they'd even noticed. She waited until they'd clambered inside their carriage, with some degree of difficulty, before darting toward Maggie.

She was feeling quite pleased with herself when Maggie peeked over the edge of the roof. She grinned and pulled her legs backward right over her head in a spine-breaking arc and dropped the painting down to Summer by her toes. "Now you're just showing off," Summer muttered.

Maggie grinned. "Well, I *am* used to applause."

"No doubt."

"People sometimes throw flowers."

"I'm all out of roses."

"'Sall right—I prefer guineas."

Summer tucked the Botticelli under her cloak and hurried back to the carriage.

Chapter Seven

T HEY GATHERED IN the pineapple drawing room just before dawn.

Maggie's face was still smeared with the charcoal and ashes she had applied to better hide her as she dipped in and out of the Collectors' skylight. She wiped at it now, mostly transferring it to her hands and cuffs. She wore rough trousers and a linen shirt under a vest. She looked so comfortable that Summer envied her all over again. Still, she was rather proud of her leather garters and her pocket still heavy with a fish-man.

Beatrix was the last to arrive, wearing the usual dark brown dress that suggested she was anyone from a lady's companion to a maid to an earl's daughter fallen on hard times. Truthfully, she could be any of those things. Her smile was a bit smugger than her usual placid reserve. Summer smiled back. "Finally, proof that you are human like the rest of us."

Beatrix wrinkled her nose. "Don't be ridiculous."

"You love revenge, admit it."

"I love justice."

"Mm-hmm." Summer felt as though she had drunk an entire bottle of champagne, for all that she had only pretended to all night.

They had done it. They had *actually* done it.

"Don't get cocky," Beatrix said. "That was only half the collection. The rest will be all that much harder to steal at the gala."

"Spoilsport."

Candles burned on the mantel, throwing golden light onto Aunt Georgie's recovered treasures. The older woman touched them gently, greeting them like old friends. She stopped at an inkwell in the shape of a large bird, marked with an alphabet Summer had never been able to decipher. "Is that a…rooster?" Maggie asked.

"Yes, we found it in Italy. Apparently, it's indicative of very fine Etruscan art."

"If you say so."

"It's…unique," Beatrix allowed.

"It's old," Aunt Georgie said cheerfully, though there was a thread of melancholy through her voice. "And odd, just like me."

"You're not odd," Summer protested.

Aunt Georgie shot her a look. "I didn't raise you to be a liar."

She had not technically raised her, except for all the ways that counted. Summer's eyebrows lifted into her hair. "No, just a thief."

Aunt Georgie shrugged. "Every lady needs a hobby."

"True."

"And I'm as odd as a chicken in a ball gown," she added. "So was Harold, rest his soul." Lord Sutherland's attention span had space for two things only: art and his beloved Georgette. He had been an easily distractable, oblivious, and kind man. And luckily for him and his title, Aunt Georgie was more than capable of running the estate on her own. Until the nephew currently kicking her out of the house. "We only bought art that made us happy—whether or not it had any other worth never mattered to us."

The display of art currently on the mantel proved that.

A rooster, a painting from Joseph Ducreux, a self-portrait of the artist pointing a finger at the viewer with the kind of smile that spoke of mischief and wine. It was delightful, not at all stuffy and showing no trace of the dignity of his family line. She could almost hear him laughing through the canvas.

There was that Botticelli, but only because one of the cherubs in the corner had an expression that could only be described as donkey-like. All teeth and ears. Summer adored it. "Why the landscape?" she asked. She would have preferred to paint the donkey-cherub. "It's rather tame and pastoral."

"It took us a little time to realize we wanted art we loved, not art other people loved. We thought of selling it, but as I gave it to him as a wedding present, he refused to part with it."

"It does not seem like the kind of collection the Mayfair Art Collectors Society would curate," Beatrix said. "If you'll pardon me saying so."

"Indeed, I'll thank you for saying so." Aunt Georgie sniffed. "Stuffy old crows."

"May they choke on their own feathers," Summer pronounced.

And then the night took a truly odd turn.

Which was saying something. An acrobat, a thief, and a duke's twin sister in the drawing room was one thing.

Four men armed to the teeth, ranging from wily to roughly the size of an ox, was something else altogether.

Aggression, hunger, slight panic all but wafted from them like perfume. Rotten, stinking perfume. The ladies paused, turned identical contemptuous gazes toward the intruders.

Aunt Georgie looked down her nose despite a faint tremble in her hands. "You certainly were not invited."

And her butler would never have voluntarily let them in. Thistle was a stickler for order. And he trained his footmen to honor the ancient family name, but mostly to see to Aunt Georgie's needs before she knew she had them.

Summer shifted so she was partially blocking Aunt Georgie. Beatrix stilled in a way that Summer knew meant her mind was racing. There were several doors and windows for escape, but all of them were out of reach. Aunt Georgie could not run. She might use her cane as a weapon on the best of days, but it was still a cane. She needed it to stand with any confidence. Running was out of the question.

One of the men sucked his teeth excitedly. They still had not spoken. It did not seem like a good sign, but Summer was more concerned with the pistol he produced from his coat pocket.

"You'll choke on that before the night is through," Beatrix promised, a hint of her true accent coming through. Covent Garden? Yorkshire? Summer still could not be sure.

"No one has to get hurt," the larger man behind him said, already noting the art on the walls, the figurines, the pineapples gleaming with gold accents. "Just do as you're told."

Summer snorted. She couldn't help it.

He blinked, clearly disconcerted. "No one said they were mad as hens. They were supposed to be asleep."

"Madder," Summer said cheerfully, even though her heart was pounding in her ears, and she felt sick to her stomach. "You should probably rethink your options."

Please, please rethink your options.

"Just give us what we want, and we'll be on our way."

"Is this about the art?" Aunt Georgie said, her voice faintly tremulous. "This is taking things a bit far, even for the Collectors. They are the ones who reneged on their word. Lord Glass is the thief, not I."

His partner waved the pistol. "Enough chatter. Stand together, over there. *Now.* And keep your gobs shut."

They stepped closer to each other, keeping Aunt Georgie shielded. "Nonsense," she muttered at them. "You stand behind me—they're not going to shoot *me.*"

Beatrix did not look so certain.

A new kind of dread iced Summer's belly.

The men began to rifle the room, sorting through the décor, pocketing the odd item that could be fenced, but they were clearly looking for something. One of them picked up an intricate ship tucked inside a bottle, shook it. "You put that down," Aunt Georgie snapped. "That belonged to my husband."

He grinned and then heaved it at the wall.

It shattered, scattering like bullets. Aunt Georgie gasped. Rage braided with the fear in Summer's belly. "That one was a footman at the event tonight," Beatrix said under her breath. "Watch him. I don't trust him even without the obvious reasons."

As if on cue, his oily glance moved over them, top to toe. Summer stifled a shudder when it lingered on her. "We *could* let you go," he said, his eyes changing. "Since we're not here for you and I've never had a lady before. Convince me."

Summer had never wanted to physically gag so much in her entire life. It was tempting. There was a certain vindication to it, but she'd lived among powerful men for too long not to know better. She did not currently have a single advantage, and as much as she wanted to claw at his pride, she did not know what he would do, beyond something she would not like.

Instead, she smiled. The sultry, spoiled smile of a lady of quality.

Beatrix sucked in her breath. "Don't."

There was no one else who could. Beatrix was not dressed like the fancy, certainly not enough to placate the oily, desperate housebreaker. Maggie still had traces of charcoal on her face. Aunt Georgie was Aunt Georgie.

That left Summer.

The Diamond.

Stifling a full-body shudder, she kept her smile questioning, attentive.

His posture changed almost immediately. Honestly, the man was an idiot.

He held a pistol to them and still believed that his dubious charm would negate that fact. As if anything could. At least the ox behind him groaned, knowing full well that her acquiescence was not to be trusted. Summer did not have any weapon on her person. Only her cleavage, the diamonds in the hair, a fish-man vase in the pocket.

It would have to do.

"Please let them go," she said. She didn't shriek or command. She'd even said *please*. If that didn't win her a role treading the boards at Drury Lane, nothing could.

She bit her lower lip, wondered if it was too obvious. He stared at her, pistol dropping slightly away from her friends. Perfect. Well, a start, anyway.

"This wasn't the plan," the ox said. "*None* of this is going according to plan. We should go."

"I want her to convince me," the other man replied, smugly. He closed his hand over her shoulder, digging his fingers into her skin. "All this soft skin and shiny baubles. These bitches think they're better than us, don't they?"

"Only because she is," a man interrupted from the second doorway, deadly and cold. She knew that voice, if not the violence currently glittering through every word. "In every way."

Blackpool.

"Get the hell away from her." The command was all sharp edges, all bloody promises. For her.

The other man froze, but his expression did not change.

The ox swore again. "This was supposed to be fast and easy."

"Shut up." His grip loosened but his pistol did not waver. The oily man was not easily cowed. Pity.

Blackpool strode forward, elegant and confident in his embroidered waistcoat, his gold buttons. He looked beautiful.

And ready to kill.

"Pistols on me," he snapped. "Not the ladies. If you're so brave, you'll shoot an earl."

Summer made a sound of protest—she couldn't help it.

"Is this what you're stooping to now? Robbing old women? Sorry, Aunt Georgie."

"I *am* old, dear boy," Aunt Georgie said, turning a gimlet eye on the intruders. "Old enough to make you pay for this. All of you."

"Let's get out of here," one of the other men said, standing in the glittering shards of the broken ship bottle. He also had a pistol, but it did not seem to be lending him any courage.

"Who sent you?" Blackpool demanded.

The intruders did not have a chance to answer.

Summer saw Maggie bend her knees in preparation. A tiny movement, barely noticeable. And then she was in the air, launching herself toward the chandelier. She gripped it with both hands and swung, aiming her heels at the group of intruders.

Beatrix went in the opposite direction. She bent low, grasped the edge of the carpet, and yanked with all her might.

The combination of the floor moving under them and the assault of legs strong enough to balance on tiptoe while on horseback sent them reeling.

The chandelier snapped. Maggie landed with a flourish. Summer darted for the service bell to wake the household as crystal burst around their ankles. Blackpool dove for one of the pistols that skittered across the floor.

By the time the butler and three of his footmen thundered into the drawing room in various states of undress, Blackpool and Beatrix both had a pistol on the intruders. They were sprawled in a heap, cursing and gasping for breath. The oily one had a gash on his forehead that bled profusely. It was rather vindicating.

"Thistle," Aunt Georgie said, sounding as though they were ants invading her afternoon tea. "Do take out the rubbish."

"Certainly, your ladyship." Thistle's eyes were wide, but it was the only outward sign that any of this was unusual, even for her.

"Send word to the magistrate and the Runners," Blackpool added, crouching down to help secure the men with the braided gold sashes that held back the curtains and a length of rough rope, which Beatrix produced, and no one dared question. "There's another thief down the hall. His head collided with the wall. Numerous times."

"WELL, THAT WAS exciting," Summer said moments later, mostly to break the silence.

Blackpool's gaze narrowed on the red marks left on her shoulder and collarbone. "He hurt you."

"I'm fine."

"I'll kill him." Something about the softness of his voice, at such odds to the words, made it a perfectly believable threat. Summer had the notion that were she to swoon or betray the least bit of anxiety, his fragile hold on his temper would break. She hadn't even realized he *had* a temper. Only charm and a smile that made people stupid.

"No thank you to your very kind offer of murder." She kept her tone light. "You can't explain what's going on here if you're deported."

Aunt Georgie leaned hard on her cane. "And there's quite enough of a mess here already," she added. "Blood would stain the upholstery."

He offered her his arm, leading her to the nearest chair. His eyes did not stray from Summer. Aunt Georgie sat carefully and then clicked her tongue. "You're bleeding."

He barely glanced at the raw cuts on his hands from digging through broken glass to grab for the pistol, and apparently from pummeling a man just down the hall. "It's nothing." He motioned to the footmen. "Get them the hell out of here and search them. Bring me anything you find, anything at all. And let me know when the magistrate comes to claim them for Newgate. I have my own questions."

The oily man shuddered at the mention of the notorious London prison. *Good.*

Aunt Georgie pointed at Blackpool. "Explain yourself, nephew."

He frowned at the art lining the mantel. "Did you steal *all* of this back tonight?"

"Of course we did. I told you that you were taking too long. I'm old, my boy."

"You're healthier than most women half your age. Not to mention twice as stubborn."

She smoothed her hair. "Be that as it may. Why are those dreadful, pompous popinjays sending ruffians into my drawing room? That seems excessive."

"But they weren't here for that, were they?" Beatrix asked quietly. "They weren't sent by the Mayfair Art Collectors Society."

Blackpool scrubbed at his handsome face. "Not exactly."

"What, then?"

"Did you steal anything else?" he asked instead of answering. "Anything at all?"

Summer folded her arms across her chest. Beatrix and Maggie did the same.

Blackpool groaned. "Please, I need to know. It's important."

"What were they looking for, exactly?" Summer asked.

"I'm not sure."

She tilted her head. "That's remarkably unhelpful."

"Believe me, I'm aware of that," he muttered. "I'm looking for something hidden inside a Greek piece. A vase, perhaps, or a cameo."

"That's not much to go on. Why don't you even know what you're searching for?"

"It's got a fish on it." He dropped into a chair. "A bloody fish. Maybe. That's all I have."

Summer pulled the little vase out of her pocket.

"Do you mean this one?

Chapter Eight

B LACKPOOL WAS FLUMMOXED.

She'd managed, after more than two decades, to finally leave him speechless. After countless horseback races, contests to see who could climb the highest in the tree over the river, or run the fastest, after competition with dice and billiards, and chess...

She had finally won.

No, not just won. Because it wasn't as though she had never bested him before, but this was different. This felt monumental. Something to brag about.

Trouble was, she had no idea what it was that she had won at.

She pulled the vase toward her chest, just out of reach. "What's going on, Blackpool?"

"It's better if you don't know."

"It's better for *you* if you tell us every single detail right now," Summer shot back. "It's my fish-man. Perhaps I won't give him to you."

"This isn't a game."

"Then stop playing."

He was frustrated enough that she would not have been surprised if actual fire had shot out of his face. It served him right. There might be smoke coming out of her own ears, even now.

Aunt Georgie poked him with the end of her cane. Hard.

"There are probably several more unsavory men after that vase," he finally said. "After anything owned by the Mayfair Art Collectors Society."

"Why?" Aunt Georgie asked. "It's ugly. And Lord Glass only bought it to vex me when I wouldn't buy that dreadful old painting from him at such an inflated price."

"I didn't know that," Summer said. "I am now exceedingly glad I stole it."

"You shouldn't be," Blackpool said.

"Why not?"

He leaned down, bracing his hands on the back of a settee. This wasn't his usual elegant leaning, meant to entice. This was a fight for control over whatever emotions were currently rampaging through him. His jaw tightened. "Because you don't know what it is that you stole."

"But *you* do," Beatrix said.

"Yes." He pushed away from the settee, seething with frustration. But he didn't offer any more details.

"Nephew, I am waiting."

They waited a little bit longer. Blackpool marched to the sideboard, poured a tumbler of whiskey, and then threw it back. "All I can say is that a great many people want it, from the War Office to the French. Give it to me, Summer. Please."

The *please* was a nice touch. She might have even let it sway her. Except she was the one who had inadvertently brought the intruders here, and she would be the one to make sure they never returned. She couldn't do that without information. Beatrix had taught her that. "No."

"Summer."

She turned her back, holding up the vase to a nearby candle. She inspected it carefully, looking for marks, scratches, anything at all. It seemed to be exactly what it was: a very old vase. She peered down the neck. Darkness. "It's too narrow and deep," she said. "I can't see anything." She shook it a little. Possibly, just possibly, she heard the faintest scrape of something inside.

"I'll get my reticule," Beatrix said, but Maggie was already handing it to her. Beatrix pulled out a blade, a vinaigrette, a fan, coin purse, and a pair of very long metal tweezers.

"Do I even want to know what those are for?" Blackpool muttered.

"Tweezing," Summer replied, reaching for them. "Eyebrows, stray chin hairs. Being a lady is not for the faint of heart."

She'd have to ask Beatrix later what they were *really* used for.

"I wish you wouldn't," he said tightly into the fraught air as Summer slid the tweezers into the vase.

"I know," Summer said. "But you're not telling us anything."

"I've told you enough."

"We both know *that's* not true. No quarter, Blackpool." How many times had they said that to each other, over games of cards or dice or wagers placed on insignificant things?

It took two tries, but finally she pulled out what her fish-man was protecting. A piece of parchment folded into a tight square.

"Give it here," Blackpool said.

"Certainly not."

She was very careful as she unfolded it. She didn't know what she expected—some sort of recipe for poison, a twist of gunpowder. A secret love letter full of scandal.

Not gibberish.

It was a list of numbers. Were they code names for the gossip papers? Illicit affairs, illegitimate children, forged wills? Mathematical equations?

There was one name, however. *Madeline Pope, the Lark.*

"You found it," Blackpool said, sounding faintly stunned. "You actually found it."

"Of course I did," Summer replied immediately. She paused. "What did I find, exactly?"

"It's a list of names." Beatrix looked over Summer's shoulder, frowning thoughtfully. "Spies," she guessed. "But you need some kind of cipher to translate it. I'm right, aren't I?"

He nodded curtly. "I am only telling you this so that you

don't throw yourselves headfirst into danger again. The Mayfair Art Collectors Society's ire is nothing to this."

"Can you read it?"

"I cannot." He sounded deeply frustrated. "Not yet. But at least we know this one copy has not found its way into the intended hands. And now we have an opportunity to break the code."

Beatrix frowned thoughtfully. "What *do* you know?"

"Only that the cipher needs to be found in order to translate it and safeguard the women listed. Before it's sold."

"The spies are all *women*?" Summer asked, delighted despite herself.

"That list *cannot* fall into the wrong hands. And the last thing you need is to be associated with it, even accidentally. Whoever they are, they would kill those women and have no compunction in killing the lot of you as well if you get in the way."

"Do you know what might have helped?" Summer asked with exaggerated care, now also thoroughly annoyed. "If you had, say, mentioned anything about this to any of us. *Anything at all.*" She was so tired of being underestimated. It stung even more when it was Blackpool. Which was ridiculous. He had never taken her seriously.

"*I told you to stay out of it.*" The silence that descended was so heavy, so thorough, he grimaced. "That sounded better in my head," he muttered.

"Eliot Howard," his aunt said. "You are not too old to be horsewhipped."

"Yes, Aunt Georgie."

He wasn't remorseful. Nor was he trying to be autocratic. It wasn't his style. Not when people bent over backward any time he looked in their direction.

He was frightened.

This wasn't a game, even though everything between them always was.

"What do we do?" Summer asked.

"You pretend you never saw a thing and you leave it to me," Blackpool replied, but he did not sound as though he thought for one moment that they would agree. Clever man.

"I'll pretend you never said that instead," Summer offered. "We can't let them have the list, obviously."

"They won't stop coming for it. As you've seen tonight. Someone's been using the art collection to pass messages back and forth. Mostly items belonging to Lord Glass. He's the only real lead we have."

Something very much like a sense of purpose moved through her. This was a worthy endeavor. A way to actually effect change in the world. To *help*.

He groaned. "I'm never getting rid of you now, am I?" He cursed. A proper curse, not the ones men used to show their exasperation. She raised her eyebrows, impressed.

"*Eliot Howard.*" Aunt Georgie sniffed. "That curse is not grammatically correct."

He looked faintly ill, then as hard as if he'd been carved from marble. Summer nearly didn't recognize him.

"What is it?" she asked.

"The Lark," he said, reading the last name on the list, which had been partially hidden under her thumb. "That's not in cipher. Madeline Pope is her real name. I have to go."

Summer grabbed her cloak, which she had dropped on the nearest chair. "I'm coming with you."

"SUMMER, GET DOWN," Blackpool said when she threw herself onto the bench of his phaeton not ten minutes later.

"No."

"I don't have time for this."

"Then stop wasting it." She grabbed the reins from him, nudging the horses into a walk. He grabbed them back.

"Summer," he said through his teeth. "You cannot come to a brothel with me."

"A brothel? Which one?"

He blinked. "What do you mean, *which* one?"

She rolled her eyes. "I could name all of the fashionable brothels by my first week of my first Season. The men of the *ton* are hardly subtle."

"I suppose not."

"And brothels are not just for men."

He went still, glanced at her out of the corner of his eye. "I beg your pardon?"

She only shrugged.

"We'll be circling back to that," he promised.

"Why a brothel?" she asked into the quiet. It was as calm as London streets ever got in that hour between the return of revelers to their beds and the early rise of workers to their jobs. The rain had stopped, but it glistened like gold under the lamplight.

"Because no one pays much attention to who visits or how often. Acting furtive or secretive is not unusual and therefore not remarkable. Prince or pauper, they all pass through the doors."

"Those men tonight…"

"Will not take kindly to a spy."

"But they were not French."

"Men like that sell to the highest bidder. King and country mean nothing."

"Is that why they added her real name? To inflate the price."

He nodded. "To prove the list is genuine, and the cipher worth whatever price the seller is asking for it."

"And Lord Glass is involved."

Summer thought about what she knew of the man. An earl, obsessed with horses, drank too much, wagered too high. Honestly, he could be any of the men of her acquaintance. He did not speak much of politics, or anything but his own entertainment. One daughter, Lady April. Poor thing. Her papa did not think much of women, or of anything but his own comfort.

"He's our best lead so far," Eliot said. "But it could be anyone from the society. Anyone at all, really. But we need a place to start."

"Why not just interrogate him?"

"To accuse an earl without solid evidence would only shut doors in my face. And I have no way of knowing it's not someone else in the War Office if it's *not* him. Or who is in league with him. But most of all, we need to nab the buyers of the list as much as we need the seller of it. More. We can't spook them too early."

"And your job is to catch him out without him knowing it."

"Yes. There are others watching the other Collectors. It's their art being used to pass messages. Could be a coincidence, but we certainly can't bank on that."

She remembered the way Eliot had looked at the cipher, tracing the folds of the paper, a furrow in his brow. The way he had always brought geography puzzles to the Tremaine country estate, riddles from ancient Roman writers or local newspapers, and puzzle boxes, always daring her to complete them before he could. She only very rarely won. She was better at beating him over pall-mall or climbing the cliffs.

"Why aren't you in charge of breaking the code?" she asked.

He stiffened. Only slightly and only for a moment. She would not have noticed if every centimeter of her wasn't already on alert. "Why do you ask?"

"Because I remember all of those hours you used to spend trying to solve ancient puzzles. And setting up new ones to test me."

"I am a rake, Lady Summer. All flash, no fire." He shrugged, tossing her a lighthearted smile she decided she hated.

And he seemed to be quoting someone. Someone she decided she hated.

She realized in that moment that he never played in the May-fair drawing rooms. London knew nothing of his hobbies.

"I'm a liaison for the Lark," he continued. "That's my job tonight."

Poor Madeline Pope. Here was a woman who was risking her

life for her country while Summer snuck about stealing paintings. While her friend Tessa took in women who were on the run from the law, or more often, the men in their lives. And while her sister-in-law Cat was up to what could only be smuggling down on the private beach of her brother's Cornish estate.

While Summer danced and attended the theater and avoided her mother.

Not this time. This time she would be the one to help.

Eliot slid her a sidelong glance as if reading her posture, her profile. "Summer, you can't just decide to be a spy because you are bored."

She stiffened. "Just drive faster."

Chapter Nine

O F COURSE HE thought she was bored.
        Why wouldn't he? Didn't everyone else?

And she was restless, no question there. But she wouldn't take a woman's life in her hands because she was *bored*.

There was no reason for Blackpool to think otherwise. They had always played games and pushed each other just to see what would happen next. He did not take her seriously. She already knew that.

But a little part of her wondered if he might.

Society treated them the same way. He knew what it was to be a doll, petted and trotted out at parties.

She'd been wrong about their solidarity, clearly. It was foolish of her to feel a pang over it.

They had bigger problems.

The brothel was well maintained, with window boxes full of white flowers and lamps burning on the steps. Carriages rolled toward and away, even at this hour. Blackpool left his phaeton in the capable hands of a boy wearing house livery. It was not so different from any other fine house during the social season.

Outside.

Inside was a riot of sound and color and sensations. Perfume, the sweet burning of candles, herbs to offset the cheaper tallow, plush cushions on every surface, and someone playing the pianoforte. Also, a very intimidating woman at the front door, armed to the teeth. She smiled a welcome, but there were still seven daggers on her belt, each sharper than the last.

Summer had only been inside a brothel once before, a very long time ago. On the last night of her second Season, she and three friends had decided to choose their own entertainment for once. No more tea with crumpets, slow walks in Hyde Park, curtsies under the stern eyes of matchmaking mamas. But she had never made it to the second floor and the chambers reserved for ladies of quality in need of a certain kind of discretion.

She'd enjoyed the thrill of being where she wasn't supposed to be, the knowledge that her mother would have an absolute rage if she ever found out. The skin on display, the laughter that was a bit too loud. But there was a hardness too, and she hadn't wanted to go any further. Her friends had disappeared in a cloud of laughter, and she had opted to play the pianoforte and turned down three offers she was certain she was not acrobatic enough to ever see through. She had still counted the night a success.

This was so much different.

Her body understood the moans floating down the stairs, the silver manacles secured to the wall, currently housing a woman with a beauty mark in the shape of a tiny black heart on her left breast. Blackpool did not even glance in that direction. He clearly knew where he was headed, and it was not the drawing room. He handed the doorkeeper a coin, only it was not gold, nor even silver. It was a wooden token, carved with a small bird. A lark.

"Bar the door behind me," he said to the doorkeeper.

Summer heard the lock engage as she followed Blackpool up the stairs. The candles were gutting out, dripping wax down the wall and onto the scuffed floor. Instead of continuing down the hall, Blackpool pushed at a small filigree on the wall, and a small snick echoed. The panel popped out. "This way is quicker, and you won't be seen."

The panel shut behind them, and the darkness was punctuated by lamps burning low in red glass globes. The passageway was well kept, swept clean, with benches set at intervals.

She soon realized why they were there. Grates along the ceiling brought a chorus of moans and whimpers and gasps. Narrow gaps opened onto lovers in various positions, pairs, groups, all writhing for the pleasure of being watched. Summer swallowed, willing herself to remember that they were on a mission for the Crown.

Her body did not much care.

Blackpool halted in front of a door and tapped a code: twice, pause, once more lower down, before opening it. The room on the other side was plain, with a bed and a chair by the fire. It also housed a desk with quills, bottles of ink, and hills of rolled parchment. More parchment burned in the grate, casting a flickering glow and too much heat.

A woman turned to greet them. She was in her mid-forties, her face plain, with a square jaw and a crooked front tooth that lent her a mischievous air despite the circumstances. Her dress was tulip yellow. "I already know," she said to Blackpool before he could speak.

"You'll have men at your doorstep in minutes," he said.

"They are already there." She pointed out the window. "Look south."

A plume of smoke hung heavy over the rooftops, brightened by the telltale flicker of a fire too big for its vessel. "That's my house," she said. "Or it was."

"I'm sorry, Lark," Blackpool said heavily. "You need to get to the docks."

"Not until this all burns. If I go, it all goes with me. That was always the plan."

"I can feed the fire." Summer rushed forward, the hood falling from her head.

Madeline raised her eyebrows. "New spy?" she asked. "Bit fancy."

"She's not a spy."

"Not yet, anyway," Summer murmured.

Madeline smiled. "I like her. Burn it all, even the edges. Nothing but ashes."

Summer turned the rolls of parchment, making sure they caught completely. She peeked, of course she did, but everything was written in code. "Shouldn't we save some of it?"

Madeline shook her head, turning to the contents of a small, hidden drawer in her desk. "I've been compromised. And so have the others, if not as publicly. Yet. We can't take the risk."

Blackpool shoved the leather satchel Madeline had already packed at her. "Time to go."

There was a sound from outside.

He glanced through the windows, down at the front of the house. "Bloody hell."

Summer shoved more paper into the flames, sweat beading her brow.

"They're here," he said. "You'll need to take the passageway and wait until I can clear them out."

"That's not good enough, Blackpool," Madeline said. "They'll burn this building down with the people still inside if they've a wish to. A hidden passageway won't stop them."

"I can stop them," Summer said, getting to her feet slowly.

Blackpool paled, but his voice was hard enough to shatter glass. "No."

"I can climb out of a window. They'll chase *me*."

"How is that *better?*"

"It's just long enough for Madeline to get away. Once they realize I'm a lady, a duke's sister, no less, they'll back off."

"These are not good men."

"All the more reason."

"No."

"I wasn't asking permission, you lummox."

Madeline nearly smiled. "As entertaining as this little play is, she's right, Blackpool. And I only need a few minutes."

"*No.*"

"I wasn't asking permission either. I have one last message

that needs sending."

"I'll do it."

Madeline shook her head. "I don't think so." She leaned closer to Summer, whispered it in her ear. She also slipped a triangle of wood into her left palm. "Will you deliver it? Miss Carmichael."

"Lord Crowther's mistress?"

"The very one."

"Of course I will."

"Tell her Tuesday by the basket stall."

"Damn it to hell, Madeline," Blackpool snapped. "Stop trying to get her killed."

"She looks perfectly capable to me."

Summer might have walked though fire for the Lark in that moment.

But she only had that moment. She was closest to the door, but it would take no time at all for Blackpool to reach her.

His gaze slammed into hers. "Don't even think about it. I will tie you to the chair."

"It's hardly the right time for that sort of nonsense." Madeline clicked her tongue, shouldering her satchel. "Make them pay, my lady."

Summer slipped out the door, Blackpool's heavy tread behind her. She slammed it shut with just enough time to see Madeline disappear into the wall. Blackpool's curses were low and could have blistered the paint from the wall. There was no key to this door, no doubt to prevent Madeline from being locked inside.

Summer didn't need a key.

She wedged the chunk of wood carved with a little bird that Madeline had slipped to her under the bottom of door. It rattled violently when Blackpool collided with it. She threw herself down the stairs and into a side room with a large window that was visible from the front of the house. Her heart raced, pulse pounding in her ears fast enough to make her queasy. The window stuck, and her damp palms did not make the task easier.

She finally yanked it open and climbed out. She pulled her hood back up over her hair and hesitated, trying to appear obvious and yet clandestine. Where were those bloody men, anyway?

The pounding at the front door echoed. Would it be too obvious if she coughed? Loudly? Spies probably didn't cough.

"Oi! There!"

Finally.

Only now she had exactly what she had wished for: two very burly, very determined men bearing down on her. Would they even pause to let her introduce herself, or would they just abduct her? Or slit her throat?

This plan had sounded brilliant in the relative safety of Madeline's attic chambers.

She stumbled to a halt. She couldn't outrun them. An iron fence blocked her from the road, and there wasn't enough space to go around them toward the gardens. She was well and truly cornered.

"Grab her," one of them shouted. She didn't recognize them, so they were unlikely to recognize her. She didn't know if that was a help or a hindrance, honestly. She didn't know how to get herself out of this.

"There you are," Blackpool said, stumbling from the shadows, sounding faintly drunk. Where had he even come from? Had he climbed the fence? Dropped from the upper window?

"Oi, back off, mate."

Blackpool snorted. "You back off. I paid my coin. You can pay for your own girl like everyone else."

And then he picked her up and threw her over his shoulder. She dangled there as his hand closed over her bottom, squeezing. She caught her breath. He squeezed a bit tighter. She forced a giggle from her throat. Did the women here giggle? Ought she moan instead?

"She's mine," Blackpool insisted harshly. His hand moved slowly, a proprietary caress.

She nearly gulped.

This was hardly the time for all of the very interesting tingles his touch was kindling. She was hanging upside down, for God's sake.

"We need to see her face," one of the men insisted. Blackpool tensed under her, bending his knees slightly as if in preparation. She shoved her hair out of her face, catching the glimpse of a knife. And another pistol.

She found she was getting rather annoyed at being at the wrong end of pistol for the second time in the same night.

She pushed her hood back. She had no idea how to change her accent the way Beatrix did. She'd have to muddle through. "Lovey, if you want a night, you only have to come back tonight. Ask for...Forsythia." Forsythia was the name of a particularly acerbic governess who had insisted Summer was going to hell for her impertinence.

The men peered at her, huffed with impatience. "That's not Pope."

Blackpool wove on his feet, just a little. "Who?"

"Never mind. Stay out of the fucking way."

They marched back toward the garden. A window opened above them. "Would you shut up? Some of us are trying to swive—Blackpool? That you?"

Blackpool froze before tilting his head back. She felt his lazy smile rather than saw it. "Osborne."

Summer ducked her head swiftly. She knew Lord Osborne. He'd once courted her friend Ophelia. He would know her instantly.

"See you've got yourself a treat." He chuckled. "Didn't know you bothered with whores."

"This one's special."

"Give us a peek, then."

"Fuck off," Blackpool returned, quiet amiability from someone who was vibrating with anger.

"Think I will." Osborne laughed uproariously at his own joke and ducked back inside.

Summer exhaled. "After all that, please tell me she got away."

"She got away."

Chapter Ten

S UMMER TURNED HER face into the wind as Eliot urged his horses back toward Mayfair. "I think all the blood rushed to my head from hanging upside down," she said.

All the blood in his own body was having an absolutely apoplectic fit. The feel of her arse in his hands, his mouth so near her skin. The danger she put herself in. The dagger. Two pistols.

Honestly, if he were the fainting type, this would have done it.

Not to mention that she had agreed to deliver a message for the Lark.

He was grateful for Madeline's work, for the risks she took for God and country. But he still wanted to strangle her. And Summer.

Even if she and her friends had already run an entire operation under his nose, one that rivaled anything he'd seen from his own superiors at the War Office by stealing from the Collectors. He was both impressed and deeply exasperated.

Desperate to touch her again. Just as desperate to put her on the next ship to Ireland.

He wanted her far away from this. From danger and intrigue and fucking traitors who could not be trusted. He wanted his aunt drinking tea and telling stories in the corners of ballrooms ruled by terrifying dowagers.

He wanted Summer.

Full stop.

That kiss had threatened to upend his entire life. His brain, his heart. His cock. All of them thoroughly obsessed. And then the weight of her over his shoulder. The softness of her curves. The warmth of her.

It was no secret he had always wanted Summer. But the thought that she might want him back was enough to have him growling low in his throat. Especially when she wriggled in her seat as though she might just possibly want something from him.

"Are you growling, Lord Blackpool?" she inquired politely as the sun began to lighten the sky, a wash of apricot in the east.

She knew exactly what she was doing. And she was used to winning.

They'd just see about that.

"Tell me what Madeline told you."

"Absolutely not."

He'd known it wouldn't be that easy. Of course he had.

"I'll tell your brother," he added.

She laughed. "Who do you think you are talking to that that would have even a chance of working?"

Just as he'd known that wouldn't work either. But again: desperate.

"Why?" he demanded. "Why does it have to be you?"

"Why not?" she shot back. "You don't think I can do it."

He slid her an exasperated glance. "Of course you can do it."

"Oh." She sounded suspicious, but also pleased.

"You shouldn't *have* to."

"No one should." She looked so beautiful in the shadows and the lamplight glow, wild as a fairy queen. "Why do *you* do it?" she asked.

"They don't usually let earls fight in wars. This is what we can do instead."

"And would you, if they did?"

He sighed. "I don't know. But this is one way I can help."

"And me as well," she pointed out.

He hated that she looked so exhilarated. More than that, her dazzle was back. He'd not entirely noticed it had faded until right this moment.

Putting herself in fucking danger should not make her glow.

He was reminded of his parents, of his mother, adventurous to her core. How else would a woman from the Colonies agree to marry an earl? She had brought that spirit with her everywhere, from the frosty drawing rooms of London to the Spanish inn where they had died when a fire broke out. His mother had preferred traveling to anything else, throwing herself into every experience.

Summer was the same in her own way. And the danger to her was just as real.

Another tactic, then.

"Summer, you have to convince Aunt Georgie to stay out of all of this, at the very least."

"I won't," she said, but she said it gently. It wasn't a push against a command, wasn't the next move in their never-ending competition. "It broke her heart to have to stay behind tonight— that's why she snuck out in her carriage. At the age of seventy-three, I might add. And she was still in better spirits than she has been since Lord Sutherland died. She went months without smiling, Blackpool."

"I know." He'd sent flowers and boxes of candies and garishly decorated hats. Macarons in every color of the rainbow. He'd driven her around Hyde Park, down to Vauxhall Gardens to see the fireworks. But her grief had chased them, nipping at her heels no matter how fast he drove the horses. "But she was held up at gunpoint tonight."

"I know," she said. "And it was awful."

A great deal worse than awful.

"I won't tell her about the message. It would only worry her. But if you truly want her to stay out of the messy bits, you'll let her have the easier ones."

"Glass isn't to be trusted."

"Do you think we don't know that?" she said, gentleness fading. "Honestly, Blackpool. He stole her collection. The Collectors did, of course, but he was the one who tried to sell them."

"He did?"

"Yes. He's a rat." Her hair had come down, and it was tangling down her back. He wanted to dig his fingers through the dark waves. "But did you see her cheeks?"

He sighed. "I did." It was all going to shit.

"They were *pink*."

"And she's been pale as milk for months," he said.

"Exactly."

"It's dangerous." But they would seek out the danger, this much he knew, even before the Lark implicated Summer. Better, perhaps, that this way they might watch where they put their feet. There were hornet's nests hiding everywhere.

"We'll keep her safe." She sounded so certain. Part of him wanted to preen at that. *Ridiculous*. He wasn't a green lad with a fondness for the milkmaid, showing off like a peacock. "You're already working on a plan, I can tell."

It was hard to remind himself when she said things like that.

Because he *was* working on a plan. Seven or eight of them. He'd created and discarded them since the moment he walked in on some miscreant manhandling Summer. The urge to punch the oily little shit to death was nearly overwhelming. He'd only stopped because the magistrate had already suggested it was too difficult to understand him with all of the swelling left behind by the recently evicted teeth.

To start with, he would sneak a new false list and the vase back into the collection. It might buy them just enough time to find the owner of the original list. He would have no reason to search out the coded version he had already sent on, and so would not know they were onto him. Just a little.

He should send the actual list to the War Office. Glass was

the most obvious suspect, but even if it wasn't him, it was absolutely a member of the Collectors, to be using their art as a vessels for his messages.

It rankled that they had not found him yet.

But if they went too hard, chased too viciously, they risked spooking him and running him to ground. They'd never flush him out in time to stop the mystery buyers from muddying the water further. And Eliot could not pose as a buyer—he did not reliably know who might already associate him with the war effort. There was clearly a leak and no way of knowing, quite yet, who it was. How it was happening. Why.

Eliot was known for being able to drink a bottle of port without embarrassing himself, and for the love letters his butler found scattered on the front step of his house for all to see. Not for anything serious. It was good a disguise as any. For light espionage, not for anything else.

He'd have to do this on his own, for a little while.

Not entirely on his own, as it turned out. With Summer instead. A twist of fate he could never have predicted.

"Aunt Georgie won't be in any real danger, not really," Summer continued. "It's not like she'll be searching the docks or climbing into runaway carriages."

"Unlike you."

"I might."

He had to grin. "Is that what you think espionage is?"

"I shall be very disappointed if you tell me otherwise."

"I wouldn't dream of disappointing you."

Something trembled in the late-night shadows between them. Summer turned back to letting the wind cool her face. He liked to think it might be with a touch of reluctance. The tip of her tongue touched her top lip when she concentrated.

Adorable.

And deeply distracting. Especially when he could not help thinking about what else that pretty pink tongue might lick.

When they pulled up to his aunt's townhouse as dawn gave

way to day, he didn't want to let her go, not quite yet. She smelled like oranges again now that the wind was not on her. She still wore her gown from the ball, with ropes of pearls tangled in her hair. He caught her chin, lifting it so that she had to rest her busy eyes on him for a moment. Just a moment. The memory of that kiss and the feel of her body against his burned through him.

Like hell was he going to burn alone.

She was used to getting her way, used to her beauty and her wealth moving people bodily *out* of her way.

He intended to plant himself right in the middle.

"This isn't the time," he said. He slid his fingers along her jaw, into her hair. Tightened. She made a little sound in the back of her throat that he wanted to hear every day for the rest of his life. "But we're going to talk about that kiss, Summer. Make no mistake."

It was a struggle for her to focus on him, and that was gratifying. He hardened against the placket of his pants. He hardened nearly to the point of pain when she suddenly grinned at him, despite the tempting flush to her cheeks.

"Bet I can find the cipher before you do."

Chapter Eleven

T HE HOUSE WAS blazingly, magnificently, pink.

Rose House might have been named for the veritable forest of pink roses that climbed its walls, like Sleeping Beauty's castle.

It wasn't.

Every inch of the townhouse was painted pink, from the stones to the windowsills to the front door. It was almost enough to distract her from Blackpool.

Almost.

The memory of that kiss turned her as pink as the house. Never mind the way he had scooped her up, the strong pressure of his hand keeping her pressed to his shoulder. Between that and the fact that she had a secret message to deliver on behalf of a lady spy, sleep was in short supply. She felt a little as if she was floating.

Blackpool had joined them for the short trip from Grosvenor Square to Berkeley Square and hadn't said a word about last night. Although if the man thought they hadn't noticed the extra weapons carried by footmen who looked more like boxers, he was mad. Summer would take the extra security. She wasn't a fool. She'd set an entire army to watch Aunt Georgie if she could.

"This house is very...very." Beatrix abandoned the search for an adjective. She looked faintly bewildered. Mayfair carried on around them as if the house had not been subject of many discussions up and down the street and all the way to the river.

"It's like being inside a piece of cake," Aunt Georgie said cheerfully. "Thank God it wasn't entailed away."

Summer could only imagine what the new Lord Sutherland would have done to it.

"Rose House is my favorite place in all the world. But most people find it...too much."

"Lord Sutherland didn't," Blackpool pointed out.

"My husband, God rest him, was color-blind."

That explained so much, truth be told.

"Lady Hayes offered me one thousand pounds to strip the paint away," Aunt Georgie continued. "Because she can see it from her parlor window, and she claims it gives her indigestion."

"And you refused, of course," Blackpool replied.

She snorted. "I offered her twice as much to paint hers anything but that boring, ghastly gray. She hasn't spoken to me since. I can't say I feel the loss."

The inside of Rose House did not disappoint.

Pale blush marble floors, magenta frames around every painting, pink damask drapes at the windows. A staid painting of a cheetah on the plains was anything but staid, since Summer had washed pink watercolor over the giant cat. Even Maggie blinked, and she was used to the circus. Aunt Georgie let out a pleased sigh and handed her bonnet to the housekeeper. "Hello, Mrs. Chadha. It's been too long."

"Welcome home, your ladyship." Mrs. Chadha was from India and had traveled to England with her father when she was a girl. He had worked for the family as a coachman.

"Thank you. Thistle will follow tomorrow. Now, these are my guests—Lady Summer you know, and Miss Beatrix Townsend and Miss Maggie Brixton. I trust you'll make them comfortable."

"Of course." If Mrs. Chadha thought it was odd that Aunt Georgie was trailing women of various social standing, she did not remark upon it. Countesses could do as they liked. Hence, pink house.

"You remember my nephew."

"Lord Blackpool." When he winked at her, the woman, white-haired and with a gaze that could puncture steel, blushed. "Oh, on with you," she added when he bowed over her hand and kissed it.

"Mrs. Chadha, I have been counting the days."

"Rascal. I see you've not changed."

Summer snorted. With feeling. He turned his wink on her. She crossed her eyes in response. His grin was quick, unpracticed. She nearly blushed as well but flatly refused to. *Refused to,* she told herself sternly when her cheeks threatened to warm.

It was just a kiss. A little touching. In the name of the War Effort.

"I think I'll lie down before dinner," Aunt Georgie announced. "And leave you all to get settled."

Summer was shown to the Strawberry Room, aptly named. Delicate red strawberries patterned the chairs by the fire, the cushion in the window, the counterpane on the bed. They were painted on the wall, on the armoire, even on the chamber pot behind the screen. She had her own perfectly serviceable townhouse not ten minutes away by carriage, but she had not stayed there for any length of time since Lord Sutherland's death. Since she had hired them, Aunt Georgie insisted that Beatrix and Maggie be given rooms as well, in case they needed a safe place to hide during the investigation resulting from their heist. And pink cushions. Clearly, everyone needed pink cushions.

Beatrix was in the Pomegranate Room next door, and Maggie in the Hollyhock Room beside her. She squealed at the opulence, then poked her head out into the hallway. "I should be staying in the servant wing, shouldn't I?"

"Lady Sutherland was quite clear," Mrs. Chadha replied.

"It's too fine for me, surely. I smell like horses and grease paint most of the time."

Mrs. Chadha smiled, softening her stern features. "Don't jump on the bed in your muddy boots and you'll do fine."

"That was one time!" Blackpool called from his own room across the hall. No surprise that he refused to leave them alone, even with the new footmen he had hired. "And I was nine years old."

"Not a spot less of mischief in you since then, my lad."

He was hidden from everyone but Summer, standing just inside the door. His eyes found hers, full of heat and promise. Mischief, as Mrs. Chadha said.

Summer shouldn't like it so much.

She summoned the exasperation no one could kindle quite like him. Instead, her ribbon choker felt righter, as though it was his hand curling around her throat. Not a threat. A dare. A promise of things she hadn't even known she wanted. Heat washed through her, and lust shot down her thighs until they turned weak.

Summer shut the door in his face before she could make more of a fool of herself.

But not before she heard the huff of his soft laugh, the touch of his voice. "That's not going to save you, plum."

When Blackpool came down the stairs the next evening, Summer was waiting in the drawing room.

He paused when he saw her, throat working. "I know when you're dressed to kill," he finally said.

"I'll take that as a compliment." She smiled at him, more pleased than she liked. "One does not go to Vauxhall in a frumpy dress."

Instead, she wore red silk with a tight and decidedly low bodice, a tempting flare at the ankles. She thought it would blend the best into the leaves and gardens of Vauxhall. She pictured herself creeping between the hedges, hiding in the lilac bushes. She had rejected pearls and diamonds, knowing now that they would catch the moonlight. She had chosen a wide velvet ribbon, hiding the mark from where his mouth had touched her throat just last night. A little secret of her own that she was enjoying far too much. She ought not be distracted. She had a quest. A mission.

An ache in places usually left unmentioned.

Her body decided she was perfectly able to juggle several things at once. Danger, intrigue. Pure, unadulterated need.

"And I can't talk you out of it?" he asked.

"Certainly not."

It took a moment to corral her thoughts back into formation. They were entirely fascinated with the crinkle of lines at the corners of his eyes. The strength of his thighs in his knee breeches.

Mortifying.

"Summer?" he pressed.

"Yes." She cleared her throat. Just a little. "Vauxhall Gardens."

That smirk of his made an appearance. And the dimple.

She narrowed her eyes at him in self-defense. Glaring at his unfairly beautiful face was much more natural. Pieces of her world fell back into place. She had a message to deliver to a certain infamous mistress.

"Why Vauxhall?"

"Why not Vauxhall? It's a fine spring evening. There's nothing more natural than a jaunt across the river to a pleasure garden. Are you refusing to be my escort?" she asked archly. She accepted her cloak from the footman and fastened it. "Very well, I shall go on my own."

"Like hell."

She could not even pretend there was not an answering thrill to the timbre of his voice, just this side of a growl. This new side of him was so difficult to resist.

"Lord Crowther is attending tonight," she said.

"Crowther, is it?"

"Not quite, but that's all you'll get out of me. Not to mention, at least three of the Collectors will be there as well." She patted his arm, sailing past him. "Shall we?"

He instructed his coachman to take them to the river, where he chartered a boat to the gardens. The night was warm, the water gleaming like black silk. Even the smell had not yet had time to turn with the summer heat. By the time they reached the gardens, the perfume of lilacs and roses overpowered the usual London smell of horses, smoke, and river.

It was a small boat, and Blackpool pressed close, keeping himself between her and the captain and the three other passengers. The bank of the Thames teemed with life, with men wading close to grab the approaching vessels. For a halfpenny they would help you across; for a shilling they wouldn't tip you over. One of them reached for the side of the boat.

"Don't," Blackpool said, perfectly polite. But his expression had them retreating for easier pickings. He offered his arm to help Summer across, lingering a little too long after her feet were on solid ground.

Vauxhall, as always, did not disappoint. It teemed with visitors, from the glittering *ton* to merchants looking for a diversion, to families who had saved up for an annual treat. There were jewels, best dresses sponged clean for the occasion, tall, crowned hats doffed with courtly bows.

The orchestra towered, dripping with ornamentation, brimming with the music of pianoforte, fiddle, and flutes. The supper boxes were tucked in the colonnade curving around it, and paintings were displayed inside the nooks where visitors took their supper of ham and champagne.

From the Orchestra to the Rotunda to the Garden walks, it was dizzying. A place where everyone came to see and be seen.

Even traitors and spies. Definitely Collectors.

A familiar warning whistle cut through the cacophony, followed immediately by a hiccup of silence and a swell of excited whispers. "This is my favorite part," Summer murmured.

"Me too," Blackpool said, but he wasn't looking at the lanterns strung over their heads from tree to tree, only at her.

Another whistle and the first oil-soaked fuse was lit. Light traveled from glass globe to glass globe like magic. Thousands of lanterns shivered to light until it was like walking between the stars. A round of applause greeted the feat, as it did every night. Summer had been visiting since she was a girl, and she still clapped her hands like a child seeing it for the first time.

Afterward, she nodded to the crowd a little to their left. "Four of your top seven suspects are here tonight."

"How do you know my top seven suspects?"

"There are seven members of the Mayfair Art Collectors who run the society. I assume you are starting there, even with Lord Glass as the obvious contender." She tugged on her glove when it slipped to her elbow. "As it happens, they are the same seven who signed that letter to your aunt, after stealing her art. I warrant I know more about them than the War Office does."

"Ah. We actually do have a spymaster, I feel the need to point out."

"We have a Beatrix."

"Fair enough." He smiled at a woman passing by, who squeaked in response, her cheeks burning red.

"Honestly, Blackpool," Summer said, but she couldn't help the fondness in her voice any more than he could help his effect on other people.

"You've been busy," he remarked, as if nothing unusual had happened. And for him, it hadn't. He was worse than a poet, with devoted followers swooning as he passed by. "And how did you guess they would be here? Beatrix again? Or another terrifying art thief I don't know about?"

"Worse. A lady's maid. I sent her out this morning to gather any gossip. Between her and Beatrix, it took no time at all. Lords Reed, Gastrell, and Dalton will be visiting. Reed with his wife, Gastrell with his sons, Dalton alone. Crowther will be with his mistress. She does not enjoy the ham they serve here, but she is very fond of music and partial to fireworks."

"A lady's maid knew all that?"

"Lady's maids know everything. They hear their mistresses talk. They hear families talk, and visiting guests. And then they talk to each other. You don't need spies. You need lady's maids."

He frowned as they circled through the crowd. "Do you think the other women on the list might also be maids?"

"You don't know who they are?"

"Madeline was my contact, and three other men who are not involved."

"It's very possible. If not, the War Office is run by idiots, I'm sorry to say." She noticed the slash of his eyebrows, the clench in his jaw. "You don't like that."

"They would have even less protection than a lady would. I don't like any of this."

She took his arm. Tried not to notice the hard muscles under her hand. "I know. Now let's take a turn, shall we?"

IT TOOK OVER an hour for Summer to smile and greet everyone who clamored to be seen with her, to compliment her dress, ask her advice on guest lists and eligible gentlemen her brother might recommend.

It took another hour for Blackpool to extricate himself from an absolute riot of ladies clamoring for his attention. She took advantage and slipped away, in search of Miss Carmichael.

It was remarkably simple. She paused to admire the same frieze, murmured the message, and her work was done.

Miss Carmichael smiled and tapped her fan to her nose in acknowledgment. Her neckline bordered on indecent, but it was nothing Summer had not seen even in the best ballrooms. She wore red lip salve much like her own. Her jewels were paste, and Summer made note that Lord Crowther was not as generous as he purported to be.

"Those are not real emeralds," Summer murmured. "You deserve better."

Miss Carmichael's clever eyes sharpened. "Indeed, I do."

The following chat was entirely unconnected to the Lark and the war, and a refreshing surprise.

Summer wandered away, only because to stay would have drawn notice.

Thus far, the skills needed to navigate espionage were the same skills needed to navigate Mayfair.

"There you are," Blackpool said, abandoning his admirers. The resulting sighs could have capsized a ship. "Where the hell did you go?"

"I found Crowther's mistress." There was no harm in telling him now that he could not interfere. "She had the most charming French accent. Not at all French, of course, but very pretty."

He stared at her. "You *spoke* to her?"

"Of course I did." She tilted her head. "You're not turning missish on me, are you?"

"Duke's sisters do not generally acknowledge the demimonde, never mind trade pleasantries with them," he returned drily. There was no judgment in his tone. "Especially in public."

"Their loss. She paid me a very lovely compliment on my hair and also advice on how to get grass stains off my slippers."

Blackpool only blinked.

"I would never have taken you for a prude," she continued, mostly because he was still staring at her. "I feel certain you have had many mistresses."

He made a strangled sound. "I haven't, actually."

"Ah, I see. You prefer widows. Tidier, I imagine."

"Summer."

"Blackpool."

"Are you trying to give me a headache?"

"Why, is it working?"

"Yes."

She grinned. "Point, me."

They followed the gravel path to the more private corners of the Dark Walk. The music and the chatter of a hundred voices was muffled by the greenery. "Did you really talk to his mistress?"

"Of course I did. And I discovered that Lord Crowther does not have an eye for jewelry, for all he gloats about it. It might be worth looking into his finances."

"Interesting."

"Admit it, you are impressed," she said.

"With you? Always."

She rolled her eyes. "You're not going not tell me I'm as beautiful as a summer day, are you?"

"I wouldn't dare. I remember that drinking game on your nineteenth birthday." Men had been comparing her to the summer season for as long as she could remember. She was the sun, the songbird, the blue sky. A rose. It was not very original.

"Your friend from school nearly died," she said. "And Callum didn't even get soused at all. As usual." Even her brother's digestion was ducal. It was a bit annoying. Especially as she had spent the next morning with her head in a chamber pot.

"And then you stole a goat and tried to get it to sleep in your mother's bed," Blackpool said.

"You helped!"

"Yes, but it was your idea."

She folded her hands with pretend primness. "I am sure you're remembering that incorrectly."

He leaned a little closer. "Actually, it was Aunt Georgie's idea."

Summer blinked. "It was?"

"I found out later. We were so foxed we didn't realize she nudged us along to the barn and even opened the doors when we couldn't work them."

"I do love that menace of a woman." She shook her head. "I can't believe Callum never snitched."

"No one crosses Aunt Georgie, not even a duke's son. She's too unpredictable. Summer?"

"Yes?"

"Don't disappear like that again. It could be dangerous."

"I know that."

"Do you?"

"Yes, Eliot. I am perfectly aware of the danger."

They both stilled. She had not called him by his name since that stolen kiss all of those years ago, long before her nineteenth birthday. She hadn't realized he'd noticed.

He'd definitely noticed that the danger she was referring to had nothing to do with spies and war secrets. She had touched the ribbon at her throat and did not realize she had done so until he tracked the movement with those dark, searing eyes. Her heart sped up entirely of its own volition.

"We should return to the main walk," she murmured.

"Conceding the field, Lady Summer?" he asked softly. "So soon?"

Chapter Twelve

HER SPINE SNAPPED to attention, just as he'd known it would. "I've never conceded to you, *Lord Blackpool*."

He huffed a laugh. "Oh, I know that all too well." Why did he sound so pleased about it? Why was he still glancing at her throat, as if also remembering the drag of his lips over her pulse? The light suck of her skin into his hot mouth. He traced the ribbon gently, and she shivered, arrested. He tugged at the bow at her nape, and the ribbon gave away, dropping to the grass. She barely noticed. She was too focused on the way he was looking at her.

He rubbed his thumb over the fading mark left by his mouth. She nearly moaned. And why was she swaying toward him like the tides under the moon? That would not do.

If she was going to drown, she would take him with her.

That had always been the agreement. No quarter. Challenge extended, challenge accepted. No matter the prize, no matter the situation.

This was no different.

This was *very* different.

Her body did not seem to care. Not one whit. Still, she turned to face him, arching her brow imperiously. Lady Summer did not concede.

Lord Blackpool teased and challenged.

But *Eliot*, apparently, was a different sort of man altogether.

How had she not seen this side of him before? The man who looked down his nose at her as though he owned her, as though he knew every tremble in her thighs, every pull of sensation ignited by his gaze alone.

He stalked toward her slowly, confidently, as though he had all the time in the world. It was inexorable, though, his approach. He was the moon to her ocean, pulling at her with invisible power. She stepped back, not through fear, but because of the thrill of it.

And the privacy afforded by the little alcove, choked with pink roses and juniper branches. He kept coming, building a sizzle of anticipation she felt all the way to the soft, wet place between her legs. She wanted to rub her legs together to ease the ache but would not give him the satisfaction.

His smile turned hungry. She bumped into the trunk of an oak tree.

He didn't touch her, not yet, merely leaned down so his lips hovered by her ear. "Didn't I tell you we'd talk about this?"

"Is that what we're going to do?" she taunted him, because she had never wanted anything more than she wanted him to touch her. "Talk?"

Her breath came short as she looked up at him. He was so much taller than she was. She wasn't sure she'd truly noticed that before. They were always playing billiards or pall-mall, trading quips across a dining table. Moving, never still. You couldn't be caught that way.

She knew she was in over her head the moment his mouth claimed hers.

And she didn't care.

Summer *always* cared. But not today. Not with Blackpool pressing against her, his hand strong at the flat of her back, pushing her closer still. He didn't tease, didn't sip at her like she was a delicate champagne.

He drank deep.

Her head swam with it. He licked into her mouth, once,

twice. He scraped his teeth up the column of her neck, and shivers of sensation shot up her legs, down her spine. She closed her hands around his arms, muscles moving under her fingertips in response. She nipped at his lip because she refused to be the only one caught in this whirlwind. His thumb traced her collarbone, dipped to graze the skin at the neckline of her dress, dipped lower to skim over her nipple. She gasped into his mouth.

He lowered his head, tongue following the same path until her breast was free of her stays and he licked it. He circled the peak, softly, then more insistently, and finally drew it into his mouth. Arrows of lust shot into her core, weakening her knees when he grabbed a fistful of her skirts and pulled them up. The soft spring air touched her inner thighs just before he did. Strong hands gripping her, parting her legs, making her gasp again. And again.

He ran his finger over her hot flesh, between the folds, slippery and aching. "All this for me?" he asked with a wicked smile. Her head lolled back when he grazed her bud. "Answer me, Summer."

"Damn it, Blackpool." She pushed closer when his touch danced away.

His other hand circled her throat, loosely but firmly, forcing her to look at him. She nearly whimpered at the intensity of his gaze, at the loss of his fingers. "That's not an answer," he said. "You're so used to everyone giving you exactly what you want before you even ask, aren't you, plum? But that's not what you want from me, is it?"

She shook her head mutely. She knew if she opened her mouth to talk, only a gasp would emerge.

"Is it, Summer?" he pressed. A glide through her folds, just a tease.

"No," she finally moaned, bucking against him, chasing that delicious build of sensation.

"Good girl." He filled her so immediately, so fully, fingers sliding into her quim until she pulsed around him. He groaned.

"Such a good fucking girl."

He was right about one thing. No one spoke to her that way. No one would dare. She would never allow it.

So why, then, with Blackpool's rough voice in her ear, did she clench and flutter, waves of want rising like that tide he was so adept at controlling? He went deeper, pinning her with his hand still at her neck, keeping her still when she thought she might have finally lost the power to hold herself up. In and out, a circle of her bud, in and out again, until he found the angle he was looking for and curled his fingers. He kept his thumb on her clitoris, circling, circling even as he pumped ruthlessly into her.

She came without warning.

It took her over completely. She moaned loudly enough that Blackpool covered her mouth so they wouldn't be discovered. So that her cries wouldn't be heard from the gravel walks.

It only made her come again, harder.

When the waves of pleasure finally receded, Blackpool stepped back, releasing her gently. Her skirts fluttered back down around her ankles. She stumbled, finding her balance again. No wonder he was so smug all of the time. He literally had women stumbling at his feet. She might have felt embarrassed, but there was no room for anything but lazy satiation, for the kind of satisfaction she'd never imagined.

And she had a very good imagination.

He kissed her again, softly, tenderly. And the juxtaposition was nearly too much. Made her want things she had no business wanting.

He was still watching her, their gazes snared together, tangled like ivy.

And then he turned his head, just slightly, tensing. That change again, from charming rake to hunter. Predator. "We should go."

She swallowed, wanting to stay exactly where they were. If they left the alcove, she would have to start thinking again. There would be consequences to what they had done, to what she wanted to do again. Could they pretend nothing had happened? Even with her knees still weak?

She nodded once. "Of course."

He stared at her for one more moment, long and delicious and somehow even more intimate than the press of his fingers between her legs.

And somehow, somehow, when they emerged from the hedges, she was Lady Summer again.

And he was Lord Blackpool.

Except…

He bent his head, every inch the flirt. "Someone is following us."

She tensed, forced herself to keep walking as if she had not a care in the world. She desperately wanted to look over her shoulder.

"Don't," he ordered her softly.

She would have bristled, but he was perfectly correct. To look around would give them away.

Blackpool escorted her to the main path, still dotted with deep shadows between the lamps, but well populated. Couples wandered by, in search of privacy. No one would pry, but everyone would notice every single detail to whisper about later. More than one assignation would be mentioned in the gossip rags come morning. They had long since given up on Summer and Blackpool as worthy of intrigue.

She had too. Before tonight.

"You'll be safe here. Don't sneak off," Blackpool warned her.

She just nodded and sat on the nearby bench, waving her fan as if she was overheated from their walk.

She was definitely overheated, but it had nothing to do with walking.

And he did not seem particularly affected. He strolled away as though in search of champagne to cool her down. To be fair, she had come so hard she saw stars. He hadn't. She hadn't had a chance to even the playing field. To see his eyes glaze over when he lost control.

Right. The playing field. This was a friendly competition, nothing more. Certainly nothing to get all flustered over. This was hardly her first flirtation. Or affair. And this was neither of those.

She didn't know *what* it was.

There were actual lives at stake. *Head in the game, my girl.* Why did she keep having to remind herself of that?

And why did it mean something else now?

A flibbertigibbet. She was being a flibbertigibbet. And it was most unlike her.

It was also very, *very* annoying.

She had herself mostly under control when he returned, mouth smiling but eyes grim. There were bruises on his knuckles. "Your reputation is safe."

"I wasn't worried about that." She dismissed the very thought. She might not know what had changed between them, but she would always know that Blackpool would never condone disrespect toward her. And she had spent years strengthening her reputation for this very reason. So that it would not shackle her.

"He won't be getting up again anytime soon," Blackpool continued.

"I had no idea you so regularly laid men out."

"He was following you," he said darkly. "He's lucky he's only unconscious. If I didn't need answers, he'd be in far worse shape, I can promise you that."

"Shouldn't you take him away?"

"He's secure until I can send someone who can fetch him. I've a man making the rounds of the supper boxes as a waiter. Shouldn't take long."

"You do?"

He glanced at her, half smiling. "Believe it or not, I am not completely useless."

"I've never thought that." The *ton* had thought it, though, she now realized. And she had not defended him. She'd been too annoyed by the way he teased her. The way he made her feel. She suddenly wondered if that had bothered him. Surely not.

"Let's get you home," he said, his gaze gone flat and lethal as it took in the visitors laughing and socializing all around them.

"Are you sure he was following us?" Summer asked quietly. "And not them?"

Not ten feet away, Lords Reed, Gastrell, and Dalton stood just inside the shadows of the greenery, speaking in low voices. They appeared to be taking their leave of each other. Lord Reed was already facing the exit.

Blackpool cursed. "This whole bloody mess is already far too complicated. I'm taking you home."

"Not yet. We're not done here." His hold on her arm tightened. She raised an eyebrow. "Blackpool."

Muttering, he released her. Reluctantly. Grudgingly. With a scowl fit for a bear. It was so honest, so genuine, and so unlike the charming mask he offered everyone else, that she found herself momentarily arrested. All of these years they had bickered and teased and competed—she'd never realized how rare it was for him to shed that façade. She'd aways thought it was because he didn't take her seriously. That she wasn't worth the effort it took to flatter and seduce.

Now she wondered.

Or she would. Later. When there was time. When she didn't have to pull her focus from wanting to lick the ticking muscle in his jaw toward espionage and treason instead.

If Aunt Georgie always said a lady needed a hobby, Summer's mother claimed a lady needed to be able to do three terrible things at once, all while smiling.

Her mother's idea of terrible things included eating bland soup at a supper party without shuddering, tripping on a fallen hem, mis-conjugating French verbs, and being able to take out a debutante from across a ballroom.

Her mother was occasionally right. Also, terrifying.

"Come with me," Summer said.

She led them through the other exit, where the drive and the road were choked with waiting carriages and bored coachmen. "We need to buy Beatrix more time," she explained. "While we are here, she is rifling through their studies. Just in case. So that we may focus more clearly on Glass, may rats eat his liver."

"You don't need me at all, do you?" Blackpool asked drily. She glanced at him, expecting censure or wounded male ego. Instead, he looked impressed. Proud.

She blushed.

She hadn't blushed when he'd plunged his fingers deep inside her, but she blushed now.

"Just try to keep up," she whispered, before she said something embarrassing. Like *thank you*. Or worse: *again*.

"I've spent my entire adult life trying to keep up with you," he muttered, and again, it was sweeter than any sonnet.

She was in very great danger.

And it had nothing to with Collectors or the war or traitors.

They slipped between the horses, with Blackpool calming them with a stroke of the nose or the flank. The coachmen were mostly gathered by the entrance, throwing dice, staying warm by the torches. Those who had opted to remain with their carriages, bundled in their coats, mostly napped. A few tried to read by lantern light. They ignored Summer and Blackpool, who looked exactly as they were: aristocrats. But as they weren't aristocrats who belonged to their carriage, it did not signify.

Summer was not particularly used to being overlooked. She found it surprisingly useful.

Lord Dalton's carriage was the most ostentatious, which did not surprise her in the least. She meddled with the traces, just enough to take some time to reattach them without harming the horses.

She met Blackpool at the edge of the cobblestone path, and they merged into a leisurely stroll together.

"How did you know they took the long way over the bridge with their carriages instead of a boat?" he asked.

"It would offend their dignity to totter about. And Lord Reed has a bad knee. The last time he tried it, he wobbled so hard his hairpiece fell into the Thames."

"Let me guess," Blackpool said. "Your maid told you that."

She smiled.

"I need an army of maidservants," he said. "Clearly."

"You do, but as it happens, I did not hear it from my lady's maid. I witnessed it myself. And then he fell right in while trying to reclaim the horrid thing."

"Lucky you to have such entertainment."

As the gentleman in question had tried to grope her backside, she counted herself lucky indeed to have seen him topple. She'd made sympathetic noises, all while hooking her left foot around his ankle. One little shift of her weight and over he went.

Blackpool looked down at her. "Lady Summer, did you push him?"

Her smile stayed absolutely serene.

His did not.

"What did he do to you?" he demanded.

Damnation.

He was more perceptive than she had given him credit for. As if he truly *saw* her. There were too many versions of him for her to keep sorted.

She shrugged one shoulder, kept her voice light. "He deserved it."

"I have no doubt, and that was not my question."

He was suddenly right behind her, pressing into her, towering over her. It sent a shiver through her. As did the gentle tickle of his breath along the shell of her ear.

"Haven't you realized by now, plum, that I will do anything for you?"

She swallowed. She had no reply to that. Not a verbal reply, at any rate. Her entire body had a great many things to say on the subject. It sang, it pleaded—it might outright beg.

And then others joined them. One of the groups of coachmen

shouted when a game of dice turned. They weren't alone. They had never been—it had only felt that way.

Blackpool shifted. He was still behind her but not as close. She could not feel his warmth anymore. She missed it immediately.

She blamed it entirely on the cooling night breezes.

Like a liar.

Chapter Thirteen

As much as Blackpool might have envied them their army of maidservants, it was, as it turned out, not enough.

The studies of Collectors in question were thoroughly rifled through and nothing untoward was found. Well, that was not precisely true. Beatrix had found several incriminating letters, and a sketch she claimed hurt her eyeballs. But nothing that suggested any interest or information on espionage.

And neither Summer nor Blackpool had overheard anything useful. Not that she had expected to, especially so soon, but it would have been nice. And then he had dropped her off and turned right around to go interrogate the man skulking around Vauxhall. Without her.

It was late in the morning, and he still had not returned.

"Are you sulking?" Beatrix asked, looking up from her ever-present notebook filled with lists.

Summer wrinkled her nose. "I do not sulk. I am the sister of a duke."

Beatrix snorted.

"Oh, hush," Summer said, but she was smiling. And sneezing.

"Bless you." Beatrix shook her head at the veritable forest of flower arrangements surrounding them. Dozens and dozens of roses, tulips, lilac branches, bunches of lily of the valley. A bouquet of flowering hawthorn branches so big it nearly touched the ceiling. Seven potted orchids. It was a bit like being under siege.

"It's bad luck to cut hawthorn trees after May Day." Beatrix sniffed. "I'm putting these outside." She dragged the pot through the French doors and out onto the terrace. "Why so many flowers? Is it your birthday?"

"No, my butler is tired of them arriving to my house every morning, and he's sending them here now."

"These are all for you?"

"I'm afraid so."

Beatrix plucked the note nearest to her. *"A rose for a rose."*

Summer ate a strawberry, entertained by her friend's expression. "Read another one."

"A rose for a rose. Again." Beatrix frowned, stretching to reach other one. "And again!"

Summer nodded. "Ever since I turned seventeen."

"That's...awful."

She beamed. "Thank you, Beatrix. No one else seems to think so."

"Whoever sends you roses knows nothing about you," Beatrix grumbled. She reached for an arrangement of spring blossoms.

"You'll hate that one more," Summer predicted.

"Shall I compare thee to a summer's day? Thou art more lovely and more temperate. Rough winds do shake the darling buds of May, and summer's lease hath all too short a date." Beatrix actually looked offended. "How many times are you sent this bit?"

"Many, *many* times. And it is recited at me at least once a week, usually with a large audience."

Beatrix stalked through the room, reading and counting. "Nine times in this breakfast room alone. And I happen to know there are twice as many bouquets in the drawing room. *Nine times."*

"They mean well." Summer sneezed again. "Though I admit, I'd prefer chocolate." She sneezed again. "It doesn't make my nose itch."

"Hmph." Beatrix poked her head out into the hall. "Would you please take all of these flowers out into the garden? You'll need at least three footmen. Possibly four." She glanced back at Summer and the stack of note cards by her elbow. "Is that why you write notes every morning?"

"An hour of thank-you cards most mornings of the Season, yes."

Beatrix looked as though she might scream. It was the most emotion Summer had ever seen her indulge in.

Summer smiled at the footmen when they marched in practically saluting Beatrix. She had that effect. "I usually send the arrangements to the hospitals. Or any house with a mourning wreath or black ribbons on the door." She winced. "I don't mean to be ungrateful. But sneezing all day gives me a headache."

"I think it's a lovely idea," Beatrix approved. "How do you feel about giving some to the flower girls? It's hard to make enough coin to fill a belly selling wilted violets."

"That's perfect," Summer said. The footmen marched away, crowned in roses and tulips. "Where's Maggie?"

"She had a performance last night. If she vanishes too long, they ask questions. But Lady Georgette went to sleep quite early. I hope she's not feeling poorly."

"She went to bed early, but she definitely did not go to *sleep* early."

"Why do you say that?"

"She likes to read naughty books and eat chocolate nonpareils to a shockingly late hour."

"A late hour? *That's* the shocking part?"

"Are you particularly scandalized that she reads naughty books?" Summer asked. "Or even a little bit surprised?"

"Good point." She poured herself more tea. "We need to search the collection before the masquerade but it's already shut up tight to guests in preparation for the gala. Even I can't get into the art spaces as the temporary housekeeper. Only the footmen and the members can."

"El—that is, Blackpool is a member."

"I know. I've already made a list of the members, the full staff, the temporary staff, and an inventory of what has already been delivered."

Summer looked at her. "When do you sleep?"

"I'll sleep when I'm dead."

"How...restful for you."

Beatrix was already on her feet and marching away on one of her self-prescribed missions. She nearly knocked over Thistle, who had arrived from the townhouse as a great hero when he brought a pineapple forgotten in the foyer. Aunt Georgie had knighted him on the spot, despite the fact that it was definitely not in her power to do so. She was already talking about having a suit of armor made for Christmas. Decorated with golden pineapples, naturally.

Thistle righted himself then nodded when Beatrix apologized, already halfway down the hall. He presented a pink platter with a single letter. "Mail for you, Lady Summer."

"Thank you, Thistle."

The paper was thick, the wax seal plain. It was not from her brother, nor from her friend Tessa. Anyone else she knew in Town would have left a calling card or used their family crest on the red wax. Curiosity nibbled at her.

She waited until Thistle had left before cracking the seal. There was nothing singular about the ink or the handwriting.

The *contents*, however...

Paragraphs about a house in Suffolk, people she had never heard of getting married, a new color of yarn for knitting. She would have thought it misdirected, had it not been addressed to her. And there, hidden in the gossip:

Mrs. Bellville wore a yellow dress to church. It was quite shocking. I can't imagine what she was thinking.

And now the weather turns and the little birds are hiding in the hedgerows again. Sparrows and little larks. They have been eating the insects from the rosebushes, and the blooms are scattered. Even the strawberries were not safe. Edward worries they will go hungry, being chased out of the garden, but I know they will rally. They are so common, no one notices them.

It has been too long since we were together. Shall we have tea? You know how I love an early morning walk, just as the sun is rising.

Yours,
Lady Edith

Summer did not know a Lady Edith.

She knew a woman who had worn a yellow dress when her house burned down, scattering larks.

Lady Edith must be Madeline. Summoning her to meet the Lark at dawn.

Another letter arrived, on the same paper, in the same hand-writing. It merely read: *The Cake House.*

The Cake House, at dawn, presumably. She could ask Black-pool. Codes and riddles were his forte, but it seemed straightforward enough. And he'd try to talk her out of it. Or he'd insist on coming along. And this one thing, Summer had to do on her own. She had to know she could be more than a diamond.

Maybe even a Lark.

WHEN ELIOT ARRIVED at the Mayfair Art Collectors Society, the butler was frazzled.

Extremely frazzled.

He bowed, greeted Eliot by name, and was altogether polite and welcoming, but Eliot had known enough butlers to notice the eye twitch, the faint sheen of perspiration at the hairline. "All right there?" he asked, handing over his hat and gloves.

"Certainly, sir."

"House is busy today," he added nonchalantly. That eye twitch again.

The drawing rooms set aside for the gentlemen to discuss art—or, more usually, to drink port and smoke cheroots under the gaze of said art—were only at half capacity at this time of evening. Too early for the theater and parties, too late to go riding or find a gaming hell. But the ballroom beyond was buzzing with activity—footmen hauling wooden crates, founding members of the society watching with narrowed eyes as their treasures were carried away.

Eliot wouldn't get back there with any real success today. And there were so many footmen—any of them could drop a message, most of them without even realizing what it was that they were delivering. He'd need a list of the staff. He had a feeling Summer's friend Beatrix already had one ready and alphabetized.

"I'll take a whiskey," Eliot told the butler.

"Very good, my lord." The man turned and nearly plowed into a footman. Something rattled dangerously in the box he held. Down the hall, Lord Reed paled.

"Be careful with that!" he barked.

"Blackpool!" someone shouted jovially from the main rooms. "We need another for this card game!"

"Not Blackpool—he's got the devil's own luck," someone else muttered. "It's not enough the ladies love him; the cards do too."

"She's not *Lady* Luck for nothing." Eliot grinned. "Perhaps later," he added, settling himself into a leather chair close enough to the door to see who passed by, but not so far from the others as to not be able to overhear.

A footman brought him his drink. There was a sideboard already set out with rolls, cuts of roast beef, boiled potatoes, hunks of cheese. Bowls of fresh strawberries sat next to a carafe of coffee in the shape of Poseidon.

This was what the War Office had recruited him for. Drinking, flirting, making conversation of no significance. The earl had to *earl*, after all.

The earl, however, wanted nothing more than to sit with the cipher and have a proper go at figuring it out. Tailing Lord Glass, collecting gossip, charming the *ton*—none of it held even a quarter of the appeal of working through a puzzle. Untangling it.

Finding that one thread that would pull all the knots loose.

"You again," Aidan said amiably, sitting across from Eliot without bothering to wait for an invitation. He was tall, with red hair and black eyes that saw too much, and he was roughly the size of an oak tree. "Didn't know you liked art so much."

"What's not to like?" Eliot signaled for a drink for the other man.

"Hmph."

"And you? Quite the connoisseur."

"I knew a lady once. She was fond of it. Her name was Felicity."

"Ah." Felicity was the code agreed upon between agents. Aidan was not here for art any more than Eliot was. They toasted each other with wry smiles.

When Glass finally arrived, already mildly soused and desperate, Eliot let himself be convinced to play a hand of vingt-et-un. Glass began to sweat halfway through the game. Eliot leaned back in his chair, sipping his whiskey in the most infuriatingly calm and smug way he knew how. The more he won, the more bored he made himself appear.

Glass was shaking. He'd already lost more than he could pay, that much was obvious. "It's not enough we're all getting robbed—I have to be personally robbed too," he muttered.

Eliot raised an eyebrow. "No one's robbing you, old man. You're just losing."

He was also counting cards, it had to be said. He didn't consider it cheating—for one thing, he needed this win for the war. For another, if Glass wasn't so soused, he'd be able to count as well. He'd made his choices.

It wasn't quite like being tasked with breaking a cipher, but it would have to do.

One of the other players cleared his throat. "He doesn't mean anything by it." He kicked Glass under the table. "Do you?"

Glass glanced up from his cards, frown freezing as he realized he had possibly accused another earl of cheating. Duels were fought for less. Names destroyed. Eliot just waited.

"Of course not," Glass blurted out. "Of course not. I expect I'm cross," he added. "This house has been broken into three times this week."

"And that was after we set up all of the blasted security," Lord Reed added.

Now they were getting somewhere.

"Security?" Eliot asked.

"All of the window bells and the trick floor. Lucky for them, my cousin is in the security business, or they'd be in right trouble, I think."

They weren't breaking in for the art—Eliot would bet his next hand on it. They were after the list, the cipher, the auction location. "What was taken?"

"A few vases, a Venetian glass knickknack." Glass waved it away. "We'll retrieve it all, not to worry. Now, are we playing, or are we gossiping?"

"I can do both," Eliot said mildly. He showed his hand and waited for the others to add their cards up. Glass swore. Viciously. And then he started to sweat in earnest. "I believe you owe me six thousand pounds," Eliot added.

Glass turned an unfortunate shade of green. Someone pushed the nearest container toward him, just in case. It happened to house a fern. Glass swallowed. "Another game."

Eliot shook his head. "I'm done for the night, gentlemen."

"You have to give me a chance to win it back!"

Eliot signaled for his hat and made a show of glancing at the clock on the mantelpiece. "You should hurry, Glass, or I'll beat you to your own daughter's debut."

Glass looked at the clock as well, swore. Brightened. "She's a good girl. She'll be married in no time. I'll get your money."

Eliot collected the signed debt vowels from him, folding them carefully and sliding them into his pocket. "How are you going to afford her dowry if you can't afford to pay one *little* card wager?" It wasn't little, but Eliot needed him frantic. Frantic men did stupid things. Like give up a cipher.

"I'll figure it out."

Eliot made sure to put on his hat at the most rakish angle. "I'll be by later to talk terms."

Chapter Fourteen

S UMMER DID NOT want to go to a debutante ball.

Summer wanted to make Blackpool's eyes go dark and hungry again.

Damn the French, anyway. Damn the war. And the English, for that matter.

Instead, she dressed in an embroidered gown with a square neckline that could only be described as dangerous. Distraction, distraction, distraction. For herself. For Blackpool, hopefully. For whoever lurked among them dancing while using a list of women spies for what could only be murderous ends.

Her lady's maid, Elsie, pinned her hair up, secured the clasp of her necklace, and helped her tug her pristine white gloves up to her elbows. "Lip salve?"

"Please." Perhaps it was a bit risqué, but Summer was known for her red lips, her red dresses. She was no miss straight from the schoolroom forced to wear demure white dresses until she wanted to scream. She did not envy Lady April Glass. White gowns were a nuisance. They announced every little indiscretion, every stolen bit of fun.

Blackpool waited at the bottom of the stairs, impeccably attired as always, in black and silver. His eyes flared, just a little. It fueled something inside her. The spirit of competition was still here, but now it was mixed up with something else. It was a thorny little rose, and she was not quite sure if she should nurture it or snip it dead at the roots.

"You look beautiful as always," he said.

She eyed him suspiciously.

He frowned. "What?"

"No empty flattery," she said, sailing past him. She was going to have to keep her wits about her. A simple compliment should not make her feel too warm. She'd been handed compliments since she was a girl, before even the parade of flower arrangements came to her door on a regular basis. They had more to do with her father, her brother, her title, her dowry. Her face, over which she had no control. She'd long ago learned to take them lightly.

"Who said anything about empty flattery?" Blackpool asked, closer than she realized. He'd moved up behind her, his breath touching the back of her neck. She tried to suppress a shiver, couldn't. She knew when he noticed the gooseflesh he'd caused. "Interesting," he murmured.

She had to swallow before speaking, which was just ridiculous. "What happened last night?" she asked under her breath.

He sent her an amused, heated glance.

"Not *that*," she huffed, as if she had not replayed the moment a hundred times since. A thousand. She'd woken twisted in her sheets, aching. "After that."

"I had very, *very* interesting dreams."

She arched a brow imperiously. "That's your own fault. You could have had so much more than that."

His breath changed, just a little. His gaze went to her mouth, back to her eyes. "Are you teasing me, plum? Because there are consequences."

She sincerely hoped so.

"What happened with our follower?" she hurried to add before a footman could overhear them. She admitted to a thrill of satisfaction at his reaction.

"Not much," Blackpool said. He smelled like soap and cedar

and a touch of amber. Her mouth watered.

She was clearly losing her wits. He was not cake. Her mouth had no business watering.

"He didn't see us," he continued. "That much is true. He didn't find us until after we'd left the Dark Walk. I'm sure he was after the list or the seller, but we can't prove it." He lowered his voice when footsteps sounded above them. Aunt Georgie would be with them momentarily. "I don't think anyone of the three from last night are likely to be the traitor, despite that. Too many alibis, too few secrets."

She made a face. "I have to agree. Beatrix didn't find anything of note either."

"I'll still have them watched." He quirked a smile at her. "Chin up. Lord Glass is an absolute rotter. I'm sure we'll find something tonight."

She brightened. "That's true."

Eliot frowned at the flower arrangements lining the hall table. "Why so many flowers?" he asked. "Spring flowers make you sneeze."

She stared at him.

"What?" he asked. "They do."

"That's true." She had the most inappropriate urge to launch herself into his arms. "But these weren't sent to me—they were sent to *you*."

"Hell. They've figured out I moved houses."

"It would appear so."

"How many bouquets did you get today?"

"Twenty-two."

"*Twenty-two?*"

She shrugged one shoulder. "It's the start of the Season. And they haven't figure out a way to send flowers to my dowry directly."

"It's not your dowry, it's *you*."

She would have argued with him, but it seemed bad form, as though she was fishing for compliments.

"I've only received six." He winked. "You win."

TORCHES LINED THE walkway to the Glass townhouse, and lamps burned in every window. Guests flowed into the house, black and white checkered marble underfoot, yellow flowers tucked into every nook and cranny. It was already a crush, the air too hot and thick, despite the perfume.

Lord Glass, handsome in a cold, uninteresting way, welcomed his guests politely, if clearly drunk. His daughter April smiled at everyone but mostly looked as though she was trying not to be sick. She was flanked by Lady Susan, who had supported her coming out, and her grandfather, Glass's father-in-law, Lord Tottenham. He beamed proudly, and his white hair was a fantastic lion's mane that Summer wanted to paint immediately. His portrait would glow.

"Welcome, welcome," Lord Tottenham boomed, shaking hands. He bowed low when Aunt Georgie stopped in front of him. "Countess," he said. "We are serving pineapple cake tonight!"

Aunt Georgie smiled. "You old flirt." She waved him away and continued on.

"Lady Summer," he continued, still booming. She'd never heard him speak in softer tones, as though there was too much joy in him to be contained. "Look at my girl, here. Isn't she the most beautiful thing you've ever seen?"

"*Grandpapa*." April blushed, but some of the tension in her face eased.

Summer smiled. "You look lovely, Lady April." She snuck a mint into the girl's hand. "Don't forget your peppermints."

April smiled. "Thank you, Lady Summer."

Blackpool trailed behind Summer, offering smiles and winks and outrageous flattery. She honestly wasn't surprised that even Lord Tottenham looked half in love already. She just shook her head and lost herself in the crowd. They had agreed to divide and conquer tonight, much as she wanted to look over her shoulder to see where he was going.

The music started with a soft swell, alerting the guests to the opening of the dancing. Couples found each other; debutantes shifted nervously from foot to foot, excited.

April stood in the center, looking deeply uncomfortable.

And no wonder.

Her father lingered in the doorway to the cards room, drinking wine and laughing with three men older even than him. They glanced toward April but made no move toward her. The younger gentlemen took the cue, if subconsciously. Lady Susan began to look as though she might start to scream like a teakettle on the boil. She was decidedly red. Lord Tottenham headed toward his granddaughter, but this was not something a grandfather could fix. Not now.

For a girl to be overlooked at her own coming-out ball, by her father and the men he was courting on her behalf, no less, was not an easy thing to come back from. And for it to happen to a girl barely seventeen and too shy to make a joke of it...

Summer was searching for a nearby gentleman she could bully when Blackpool strode forward, calm as you please. He bowed over April's hand. "You were too kind to wait for me, Lady April. My tardiness is inexcusable."

The others murmured, nudged each other. More than one lady fanned herself rather vigorously. Blackpool was unjustly handsome and charming, but more than that, he was *kind*.

Summer watched him tease smiles out of the girl as they paraded in the first line of the dance. She found herself smiling as well.

She genuinely *liked* him.

"You look as though you've just bitten into a pickled herring," Lord Haywood said, coming up behind her.

Chapter Fifteen

S HE *FELT AS* though she had just bitten into a pickled herring.

Liking Blackpool would *not* do.

Lord Haywood bowed, handsome in a way that made him appear to have been cut from marble. The white of his cravat glowed against his brown skin. "Shall we dance, Lady Summer?"

She took his arm. "A pleasure, Lord Haywood."

He was a decade her senior, a confirmed bachelor, and a consummate flirt. They enjoyed each other's uncomplicated company and had for many years. "When are you going to marry me, my darling?" he asked, as he always did. It was a touch too loudly, just enough to rouse attention. Even Blackpool glanced over his shoulder, eyes narrowed.

"Beast." Summer laughed. "Now look what you've done."

"No one's talked about me all week," he complained. "Can you blame me?"

She rolled her eyes.

"And you still haven't answered my question."

"I'll marry you just as soon as your proposal is genuine."

He winced, played at being wounded. "You are sharp as Stilton."

"Sharper." She wrinkled her nose. "And did you just compare me to cheese?"

"Who doesn't love cheese? And I do love you, you know."

"I am very lovable," she returned, laughing. He loved a Mr. Lawrence, in point of fact, and would not marry anyone else. She had spread false gossip about herself and Haywood more than once when suspicions were raised and would happily continue to do so. "What are you doing here?" she added quietly. "And why are there so many old men about?"

"Did you just call me old?"

"You called me cheese," she reminded him unrepentantly. "Wormy cheese, in fact."

He muttered something under his breath.

"I heard that." She hadn't.

"Glass is casting a wide net for suitors for his daughter."

"The girl is seventeen and has been out all of two hours."

"He's desperate. Gambled it all away, didn't he?"

"So he's looking for someone else desperate enough for an heir to accept a small dowry." Not unusual. There were dozens of such marriages being brokered right now, she was sure of it.

"Mostly, he's hoping for a wealthy merchant looking for ties to the aristocracy, but we're not supposed to notice that."

Motive.

"He's selling her." She was absolutely going to go through Glass's personal things before the night was through, and she was not going to be gentle about it.

The music tapered off, and the dancing came to a halt in a flurry of curtsies and bows. Blackpool escorted April back to her chaperone, and Lady Susan nearly kissed him on the mouth right then and there.

Honestly, the man was a menace.

"Gor, Blackpool looks like he wants to murder me," Haywood said.

"Don't be ridiculous."

"I'm suddenly desperate to play a hand of whist."

"You hate whist."

"Discretion is the better part of valor and all that. Ta!"

"Coward." She laughed after him.

"I like my limbs where they are, thank you very much," he tossed over his shoulder as he hurried away.

"And that's why I won't marry you!"

"I'm quite devastated."

"I can see that."

She refused to explain herself when Blackpool reached her, raising his eyebrow. Someone sighed behind her. "You have a twitch," Summer told him blandly. "Left eyebrow."

His mouth also twitched in response as he fought back a smile. A tiny one. The one he reserved for her. Oh dear, that wouldn't do either. She shouldn't have noticed that. It shouldn't make her want to smile back like a besotted fool. She didn't do besotted. Neither did he.

The orchestra began to play again from the dais wrapped in yellow roses. Dancers floated onto the floor. Lady April did not. "Look at her, red as a beet," a young man said behind them. His friends snickered.

Blackpool turned, looking down his nose at them in a manner that could only be described as threatening. "Gentlemen," he said with that smoothness she was beginning to see through. "Lady April is the guest of honor, and as such, you will endeavor to make certain her dance card is not empty."

"She stutters," one of them complained. "And she's a mouse."

Blackpool's smile went flat. The young man swallowed, throat bobbing. "You will never say an unkind word to or about that girl."

"Of course, but—"

"Fancy becoming a member of White's? Boodles? Buying a horse at Tattersall's? Boxing with Gentleman Jackson?"

All things every young fellow assumed as his birthright as a man-about-town.

They paused but were but were not quite convinced his veiled threat was something he could follow through on. "How about the Faunus club?" he added, naming an exclusive gaming hell. "Or the Lily Garden?" An even more excusive brothel than the one they had snuck into to find Madeline. "Am I making myself quite clear?"

"Yes, Lord Blackpool."

"And if that's not enough," Summer put in, "he'll seduce your mothers. He's very good at it. Wives, future fiancées. I shouldn't risk it if I were you."

They exchanged looks of horror before bowing like marionettes with cut strings. They proceeded to stampede across the dance floor toward April. The poor girl looked ready to hide behind the nearest ornamental tree. Small wonder.

"Summer," Blackpool sighed. "You are not helping my reputation."

She grinned. "I'm afraid there's no help for it, my lord."

"You'll pay for that," he murmured.

"Threats, threats," she said airily. "And yet no follow-through." She tsked like a disapproving governess.

When he turned very slowly to meet her gaze, need sparked throughout her body. "Is that so?"

Her breath actually caught in her throat. The taunt burned between them.

"Careful, plum, or we'll start a new game."

Yes, please.

Or *no, thank you.* Yes, surely that was what she meant.

Not even a little bit.

She licked her lower lip, could not help herself. He tracked the movement, eyes darkening. The music swirled around them. She felt like she was dancing even though she was standing perfectly still. "Glass is busy in the card room," she blurted out. "I have to go."

It was absurd to think that he would just let her. Still, she wove through the crowd, smiling at friends, handing her champagne glass to a footman. She chatted and socialized her way right out the doors, into the hall and down toward the darker parts of the house, generally off-limits to the party.

Not that it stopped her. Or Blackpool.

"Go away, Blackpool," she said, hearing his footsteps behind her. The wall sconce threw a little light, and many long shadows, at her feet. "I'm investigating."

"That's not your job, actually."

"Don't be tiresome."

"Tiresome, is it?" He was crowding her again, making every inch of her skin sing.

She very, very much wanted to push back against him, to see what he would do. To feel his hardness against her bottom.

She didn't. But it was a near thing.

Very near.

She was grateful to be distracted by the painting hanging by Lord Glass's study door. It was spectacularly ugly. The poor horse looked very uncomfortable, embarrassed to be trapped in such a dreadful piece of art. His legs were too long and muscular for his body, his mane an auburn not generally found in nature. There were flowers braided into it, which did not help as much as the artist might have hoped. A very large moon hung in the sky, vaguely menacing. Like a giant, ghostly eyeball. The tiny bronze plaque below read: *The Red Mare.*

"Well, that painting is just atrocious," Summer said. "They deserve each other."

"Just come on." Blackpool urged her inside the dark study. Torchlight flickered outside the window, just enough to stop her from tripping over the furniture. She had expected something far more ostentatious, gilded chairs, gleaming crystal.

"He really is in debt," she murmured. She looked at Blackpool pointedly. "That is surely sufficient motivation to sell a list of spies."

"Might be."

"You don't sound convinced."

"More than half the earls and viscounts in England are up to their eyeballs in debt."

"True," she was forced to admit.

She sifted through the papers on the desk, skimmed ledgers

and account books. Glass really was terrible at cards. And she could see at a glance that his cook was stealing from him.

Blackpool opened the leather-bound books on the mantel. Poetry, an old copy of *Debrett's Peerage*. Not much else. He ran his fingers along the shelves.

"What are you doing?" she asked.

"Looking for levers for a secret door or cupboard."

She held her breath as he continued. Nothing. "He would never be that interesting, I suppose," she said, disappointed.

The study was tidy, a bit sparse, and utterly unremarkable. It either made him a very good spy, or not whom they were looking for. Summer frowned. "I don't see his art collection anywhere."

"Is this not it?" Blackpool motioned to three vases, a Roman bust, and a small etching. "And your favorite horse out in the hall, of course."

Summer shuddered. "I'm stealing that horse for Aunt Georgie," she said. "Just not tonight."

"I admire your restraint."

"Anyway, that is not his collection. Certainly it's nothing the Collectors would display at the gala, and so useless for the passing of secret messages."

"How do you know?"

"Beatrix made a list of the items in Collectors' personal collections. She copied it from the ledgers at the house the night of the private exhibition."

"I'm going to need those lists."

"Good luck convincing her to share. She is rather proprietary." Her eyes widened suddenly. "What if he's sold the lot already?"

"Is he likely to? The man likes attention."

Her shoulders relaxed. "That's true. If he's behind the list, he would need them at hand to send and receive messages. And if he's not, he'd probably still wait until after the gala to fetch a better price. Maybe he's already had them packed away for delivery?"

"Perhaps."

"I can find them. Leave it to me."

Blackpool winced. "You've got me terrified again."

She patted his arm. "Is that any way for a spy to act?"

He groaned.

She patted his arm again.

"That is not comforting," he pointed out drily.

"Goodness, you are fractious tonight."

"Summer," he growled. A clear warning.

She only laughed.

If another hot curl of awareness tingled in her belly and her thighs at his tone and the lethal cut of his gaze, no one had to know about it.

SHE WAS A fucking marvel.

It was a struggle not to tell her that. Right now. Tonight. Every night.

But if he started, he'd never stop. And he knew damn well she would take it as encouragement and race headlong into danger.

She was a gentlewoman incarnate: elegant, confident, beautiful. But also sultry. Clever. Stubborn.

Reckless.

Why had he never noticed that wild streak in her? He'd thought it merely a part of her competitiveness, part of the way they had teased each other for years now. He'd never truly seen the desperation behind it. As if she felt caged.

It terrified him not a little. He hadn't been exaggerating. A woman such as her might do anything if she felt trapped. By Society. Her family. Her life.

Please, God, not by him.

He had already seen the change in her when she returned from Lady Tessa's house in the country. Thoughts racing behind those green eyes, faster than the wind at sea. It put him on alert, had the hairs lifting on the back of his neck. And then she threw herself into caring for his aunt, cajoling her out of the doldrums, helping her with the move in residences. Descending into outright criminal activity to bring her comfort.

He'd have loved her for that alone. As it were, it was just one more reason on an impossibly long list growing longer by the second.

And now this.

She'd have done her part regardless of the spies on that list, but now knowing they were women would make her unstoppable. Even more reckless.

And now she would absolutely skulk through the private rooms of earls and marquesses and dukes. Through their studies and their bedrooms. The Mayfair Art Collectors Society might not be particularly dangerous, but the traitor who moved among them was.

The thought of her in peril made him physically ill.

Sweat gathered on his spine, and she was right there in front of him, safe as houses. She'd already been at the wrong end of a pistol. He already knew she was perfectly capable of taking a man down, by smile or fist or kick to the kneecap. But pistols couldn't be smiled away. Punched at.

If she thought he was letting her out of his sight, she was mad.

He followed her down the hall, and the lamps gleamed off portraits of Glass ancestors. They were all very pale and could have done with more outdoor exercise. "Gah," Summer muttered. "That one's eyes are following me. Definitely a Glass."

He scowled so hard he was surprised he had not done himself an injury. "Has Glass...insulted you?"

She snorted. "His existence is an insult."

"Summer. You know what I mean."

She shrugged one shoulder, and it was so nonchalant that he wanted to punch every Glass ancestor watching them. "Glass is a rotter—you said so yourself. But he's not much different than the others like him, not more dangerous, not less. He is all hands, though."

Eliot went hot, then cold. "I beg your pardon?" His voice sounded wrong even to his own ears. Too soft, too smooth, too harsh.

She glanced at him. "Never mind him. I can handle an earl with wandering hands."

His left eye began to twitch. She looked sympathetic. He wanted to burn down the house around them, and she looked at him sympathetically as if he didn't understand the world.

"Blackpool, this is Mayfair."

"Doesn't make it right." The wash of fury made him feel like was grinding stones between his back teeth.

"On that we agree."

"He won't talk to you again, and he sure as hell won't touch you. Or any woman." Hard to touch what wasn't yours to touch when your hands were broken. And your wrists.

"You can't attack him helter-skelter."

"I think you'll find I can." There would be nothing haphazard about it.

"I mean, you can't do that *yet*."

"Why the hell not?"

"We can't spook him, Blackpool—you said so yourself. We need him to think we know nothing about him."

They had barely begun, and he was ready to burn Mayfair to the ground. God help him but he would, for her. Every damn time.

Two footmen hurried toward them, and instead of darting into the nearest parlor, Summer smiled at them. One of them swayed slightly on his feet under the onslaught.

"The trick is acting as though you belong," she told Eliot in undertones. He didn't point out that he already knew that, seeing as he worked for the War Office. She was too fiendishly adorable. And she would definitely plant him a facer.

The truth was, she was very good at it. She exuded the confidence of an aristocratic lady, and no one thought to confront her.

When she spoke again, it was louder and to the maid coming up behind the footmen with a basket of sewing supplies for dropped hems and stained gowns. After their conversation, he knew exactly why Summer had chosen her. The women in the household were far more likely to turn a blind eye to anything that might cause Lord Glass a bit of trouble.

"Excuse me, we were looking for Lord Glass's art collection?"

The maid paused as the footmen continued on their errands. "The earl keeps his treasures in the blue parlor, my lady," she said. "But it's locked up for the evening."

"A pity," Summer murmured. "I was promised a tour before the gala. You wouldn't happen to have the key, would you?"

"I'm afraid I don't." The maid curtsied before leaving. Summer sighed.

"I have the key," Lord Tottenham boomed from behind them. For a man with so much hair and such a loud voice, he moved quietly.

Summer startled but covered it with a pleased smile. Blackpool was so proud of her it was almost painful. He forced himself to appear as expected: flirtatious, carefree. A rake of rakes. It was tedious sometimes, but it did the trick. He'd learned it so long ago he barely remembered not having a selection of smiles to choose from like cutlery at a fine dinner. Or weapons.

His father might have been an English earl, but his mother was a French-Micmac woman from New France. Title and wealth was more important to Society, but it wasn't everything. Not if you gave them a single reason to overlook it. He'd learned that at Eton, where boys were spoiled and cruel and just the absolute worst. Summer's brother Callum liked to say that Eliot had saved him from the social horrors of school. Even Summer claimed that her brother needed a little chaos in his life, but as she was not allowed at Eton, Eliot would have to do. But the truth was Callum had helped him right back. He had saved him from a bully that first year, as British boys did not braid their hair nor wear it long the way his mother had taught him. Callum kicked the rotter right in the stones—and as he was a future duke, no one was brave enough to reprimand him. He'd then grown his hair longer than was fashionable.

Eliot always wondered how his mother was treated when his father was not around to object. She had told him stories of her own family: his grandfather who fished in the sea and hunted caribou; his grandmother who taught her how to gather cedar and boil it for winter fevers. How tobacco was offered to the spirits. How Englishmen and Frenchman took what they wanted with very little concern for anyone else. She always said that falling in love with a very proper British earl was one of life's great mysteries. But she said it with a smile. Her love of adventure and travel had kept his parents on the road. An inn fire claimed them far too young and now there was no one to tell him those stories.

"I was promised a tour," Summer confided to Tottenham.

Eliot smiled at the old earl with the extravagant whiskers, aiming for slightly bored but indulgent. "Lady Summer is somewhat of an artist."

Oh, he'd pay for that patronizing remark.

Still, it worked. Tottenham's grandfatherly face creased into a smile. "I admit I find my son-in-law's art collection dull as tombs, Lady Summer, but I'd be happy to procure the key and give you a tour."

"You're very kind."

"Why don't you come by for tea with my granddaughter tomorrow afternoon?"

Clever man. Having the twin sister of a duke pay you a call the day after your coming-out ball was a social coup. Whatever awkwardness April might endure tonight was about to be forgotten. Summer's smile warmed. "I'd be happy to, Lord Tottenham."

"Until tomorrow." He bowed. "You should hurry back and enjoy the strawberry creams before they're all gone. My son-in-law is a bit of a skinflint, and there are never enough."

"It's my very next step," Summer assured him.

She waited until he was out of hearing distance before smiling smugly up at Eliot. "And that's how it's done."

Chapter Sixteen

UPON RETURNING TO Rose House, Summer fled into the dark seclusion of the garden.

She needed to think. Or *not* think.

She needed *something*.

When Blackpool found her, she told herself she wasn't hiding. Not from him or the heat he sparked under her skin. Nor was she waiting for him.

He really *was* turning her into a liar. She felt out of control, unmoored. Hungry.

She found herself between two pall-mall hoops in the secluded grassy alley at the edge of the garden. She needed to sort through her thoughts. Needed to let off some of the energy coursing through her. She smacked the boxwood ball as hard as she could, just for the satisfying thwack of the mallet on wood. It missed the iron hoop completely.

"Midnight pall-mall?" Blackpool said from the darkness.

She paused. Whacked at another ball. Missed it again.

"Your aim is still terrible."

She narrowed her gaze at him. This, at least, was common ground. "Care to make a wager?"

"At pall-mall? Are we betting for hazelnuts?" They'd been ordered to use hazelnuts instead of coins the day Callum went into his private dressing room and found his locked box of coins entirely empty. They'd spent it on setting up an obstacle course through which to race chickens.

"You're right. We should make it more interesting." She felt reckless. Spinning without a center. "Every time you miss the hoop or lose the turn, you must remove an item of clothing."

He went still, except for the muscles in his throat as he swallowed. "And you?"

"Same rules apply." She tried to say it airily, not at all as if anticipation threatened to make her giggle. Or whimper.

"Summer."

"Blackpool." She mimicked his rough tone, all serious and suspicious. "Do you forfeit?" If she had a penny for each time they had said that to each other over the years, she could buy England.

He narrowed his eyes back at her. "No." He reached for a mallet, not breaking their gaze.

And then he hit the ball without looking at it, and the blasted thing rolled perfectly along the lawn and sailed through the hoop.

She hissed out a breath. "You..."

Then he turned around and did it again through the second hoop at the other end of the lane.

"Fine," she said. "No quarter, then."

"When have we ever given quarter?" he asked, amused.

True enough.

She marched up the next ball, trying to be more strategic. There was not much light, and the way he leaned on the mallet was distracting, all leashed power, controlled grace. If she didn't send the ball through the hoop in a single stroke, she lost the turn.

No one ever managed it in one swing. Never mind twice in a row.

He watched her, and it made her feel better, powerful, even, to realize he was not unaffected. She pushed her bottom out slightly, gave it a wiggle. He cursed under his breath. She grinned. "Hush, I'm concentrating."

"You are a menace."

"That's not very sportsmanlike."

"Neither are you," he added drily.

She missed.

Of course she missed. It was still a passable shot. She could make the hoop in three strokes, two, maybe. Nothing to wince over. But still not as good as his had been. When she turned toward him, he was still leaning casually, but his fingers were tight around the handle. There was effort behind his lazy patience.

She could remove a slipper, a glove. But that wasn't the game, was it?

In for a penny, in for a pound.

She removed her left stocking. Slowly. She lifted her foot, placing it very delicately on the stone bench beside Blackpool. She drew up the hem of her cherry-red gown.

"Summer."

She glanced at him with false innocence. "Yes, Blackpool?"

His jaw clenched.

"No quarter," she reminded him, enjoying herself immensely. She untied the red ribbon securing the stocking at the top of her knee and rolled the silk down. It was still warm from her skin, and the stone was cool under her toes when she draped it over the bench. "Your turn," she said as his gaze raked her bare leg.

Sometimes losing felt very much like winning. Who would have guessed?

The ball hit the iron, rang it like a tiny bell.

It did not go through.

Summer smiled.

Blackpool reached for his cravat, unknotting it with a deft tug and dropping it onto her discarded stocking. She could see all of his throat now, and a good portion of his chest as his linen shirt gaped slightly. Muscles, a hint of hair.

"Summer?"

She realized by his tone that it was not the first time he had said her name. "Hmm?"

"Your turn." There was a fondness under the reminder, and it was addictive. She wanted to lean into it. Wanted to wrap it around herself.

She took up the mallet. Swung it too hard, too blindly. It took three hits to sail the ball home.

It took him four.

Another stocking, his shirt, her dress. They all sailed into a pile, a trophy of sorts. She finally stood in her chemise, knowing he could see the outline of her legs, the curve of her hips, the pink of her nipples through the thin muslin. It was like wearing a cloud.

And it was still too much between them.

Honey gathered between her legs, made her squirm. She wasn't sure if she'd made a mistake or the best decision ever. It was too late to turn back now. She physically could not make herself stop staring at him. He was as beautiful as she'd imagined. More beautiful.

There was strength to him, hair dusting his chest and arrowing lower, scars on his legs from what she assumed was a horseback riding accident. It made him more human. It made her desire sharper, hotter.

She was supposed to feel like they were back on charted territory. A challenge, a silly game, competition.

She most decidedly did not. But if she was going to fall, she was going to bring him with her.

She knelt in the soft grass, looking up at him, reaching for his hips. He stared down at her. "I know what you're doing."

"Do you want me to stop?" she asked innocently, brushing her fingertips over the buttons of his smalls.

"Hell no," he said roughly.

And then he couldn't say anything at all.

His smalls fell down his strong thighs and she took him into her mouth with one long suck. No teasing, not yet. He cursed, low and vicious, and she smiled, sucking harder. She dragged her tongue along the underside of his shaft, up, swirling over the head. He tasted like heat and soap. His fingers tangled in her hair, helplessly, before tightening. She loved every groan from his throat, every filthy word he spoke like poetry. She cupped his ballocks, and his hips stuttered.

And then he was stepping away, jaw tight, muscles in his thighs bulging. She wanted to bite them. She wasn't finished. *He* wasn't finished.

He moved so fast that she barely had time to reach for him again before he was kneeling in front of her. He thrust his fingers into her hair, tightening at her nape, forcing her face up to meet his searing gaze. Her nipples, already throbbing, pebbled. "I know what you're doing," he said again. "You think that if you can control this thing between us then you won't get burned. But I think it's too late." His breath ghosted over her skin. "And aren't you tired of being in control of everything all of the time?"

She hadn't thought so.

Until this very moment.

He kissed her with a hunger that nearly undid her, nipping at her lip, slowly licking at her tongue until she whimpered. He pressed her backward, pinning her with his body but only for a moment, not nearly long enough. She wanted the weight of him, all of it. Wanted him over her, on her, inside her.

If this was her attempt to get these feelings out of her system, to control herself, it was not working.

He kissed his way down her body, sucking at her nipples, biting her hipbone, fingers dimpling her skin. "Do you have any idea how long I've waited to get my mouth on you?" he said against her thigh.

And then there was no more waiting.

He pushed between her legs, keeping them apart with the breadth of his shoulders as his mouth descended on her most intimate flesh. He dragged his tongue between her folds, back and forth, tasting, teasing, until she was begging. He licked her like an ice, as if she were delicious. Pleasure tingled through her, and she chased after it, helpless. "Come for me, plum," he demanded.

Demanded.

And she obeyed.

It was possibly the first time she had ever obeyed anyone. The force of her climax shuddered through her, arching her back, stealing her voice, and giving back only whimpers and moans. The tremors of her release were still moving through her when he loomed over her, eyes gleaming. Covering her with his body. "Open your legs for me, Summer."

They fell open. Eagerly. Desperately. She didn't care. She just wanted more. He nudged her entrance. Just a nudge. She pushed back, trying to draw him in. When he didn't move as quickly as she wanted him to, she reached between their bodies. They had always pushed and teased each other for a reaction, so why not now, when she was dizzy with the need to feel him everywhere?

"Still trying to orchestrate?" he asked, drawing her arms back, pinning her wrists against the soft, cool grass.

It only aroused her further. She writhed, not knowing what to do with the hot energy pulsing through her. She struggled lightly, just to feel him push back. "Eliot," she whimpered.

"Tell me what you want," he ordered her, rough and ragged, in her ear. She tried to rub against him, to pull him closer with her legs, but he was stronger. Ruthless. She whimpered again. "Tell me, Summer." He bit down on her earlobe, and every part of her was so alive she jerked, so close to coming again. "Tell me and you can have anything you want."

"I want you," she moaned against his mouth. She sucked his lower lip, hard. He growled. "Just you. *Now.*"

He stilled, and she made a sound of frustration. "Giving orders, Summer?"

She swallowed. She was so wet for him that she might melt away completely.

"Now I think you'll have to beg."

"Blackpool!"

"Eliot," he demanded against her mouth. "When I'm inside you, you call me Eliot."

"Then be inside me!" She moved under him, feeling as if she might come apart into pieces.

"Beg," he whispered in that voice of steel and stone so few people ever heard. It was a gift, a trade of vulnerability for vulnerability. And it did things to her insides.

Hot, soft, impossible things.

She still didn't want to beg. Giving in wasn't in her nature. But there was something molten in her center, something that wanted to tease and push, knowing someone else might carry the weight of it for her, for a little while. Might want her even when she was not the Diamond.

"Well?" he asked, as if she wasn't sweating against him, as if he weren't so hard his arousal dug into the crease of her thigh, dragged through her folds, relentless.

"Eliot," she finally said. "Please."

He was satisfied with her response. Which was a surprise, even to her. She was just as likely to kick him right in the arse with her heel. Which she considered.

But this, as it turned out, was more fun.

He smiled once, and it was nothing like the Earl of Blackpool's smile—nothing polite or smooth about it. It was perfect. She wanted to eat it like cake.

And then he was sliding into her, filling her completely until she gasped. He withdrew, slowly, so maddeningly slowly. Entered her again, just as slowly. She lifted her hips, squeezed him with her intimate muscles until his thrusts went harder, deeper. Their moans made a kind of primal music, urging them on, pulling at every sensation. They sounded delightfully debauched even to her own ears. Her wrists were still pinned, her spine cradled by grass, London moving all around them as if the world wasn't washing away completely, like a painting left in the rain.

They were reduced to sounds, sensations, eyes clashing fiercely as their releases rocked through them. They stayed that way, locked in the moment, Eliot's breath ragged in her ear, his arms bracketing her gently. When he lifted his head to look at her, Summer was almost afraid to meet his gaze. She didn't want to leave this pocket of time, this secret corner where the rules hadn't been made yet, not really.

"Don't," he said quietly when she glanced away. "Don't go."

He kissed her so gently, so thoroughly, that she had to clutch at his shoulders to keep from spinning away entirely. When he pulled back and rolled away it was only to find his cravat, and he plucked it from where it had snagged on a rosebush. He used it to tidy her up, and then pulled her to her feet.

If she didn't want to ruin this, she was going to have to say something. When she saw a flash of uncertainty on his face, so quickly hidden, she clutched his hand. She chose a smile, something cheerful, conspiratorial. They were nothing if not conspirators.

His lips quirked; hair fell over his forehead. "I think we might have scandalized the hedgehogs." Aunt Georgie insisted on feeding them, and they waddled through the gardens, quite secure in their station.

"Good for us," she said, pulling her chemise over her head. She followed with her gown, leaving off her stays. She felt sore and replete and happy.

Eliot pulled on his breeches, tucking in his shirt. He folded his coat over his arm. "I think I can safely say—"

A torn bit of paper slipped from his pocket and floated down to the grass.

Summer watched him pick it up. "A love note?" He must have pockets stuffed with them. She waited for the jealousy to rake its little claws through her, but it never did. This was Eliot. He wasn't cruel or manipulative. He couldn't help his charisma any more than he could help his pretty face, like something out of a Botticelli painting. Men and women alike chased him through ballrooms and crowded sidewalks and country house parties. But she was the one standing with bare feet and tousled hair at his side.

Tonight, right now, it was enough.

He barely looked at the note before crumpling it and throwing it into the hedges. He offered his arm, as if leading her into a promenade in a ballroom.

They snuck into one of the side doors, shoes in hand, moving silently. She had no wish to be caught out by Beatrix, who would have questions. Or Aunt Georgie, whose questions would be even more inappropriate. Best not to complicate things.

Not if she wanted another night like this.

And seeing as she was not dead, she most definitely wanted another night like this.

Several more nights. A hundred.

All of them.

But that was a problem to worry over later.

They crept up the stairs like naughty schoolchildren, grinning and wincing when a step creaked underfoot. When she reached her bedroom, he said her name. Simply, softly. "Summer."

She turned and was in his arms before she knew what he was about. He pressed her back against the door, gripping her hip, slanting his mouth over hers. This kiss was quick but scorching. A claiming.

It scrambled her wits. She stared at him, a bit bemused. He reached behind her to open her door, his smile amused. "Good night, plum."

Chapter Seventeen

ELIOT DID NOT sleep much. When Summer insisted on sleeping in her own bed, he wanted to convince her to stay. Demand, beg. Whatever worked.

Instead, he spent the rest of the night staring at the damned list until his vision blurred. The code was probably a book, the numbers corresponding to pages, chapter, or letters. All three. It was the most common way of coding. But even such a simple cipher was unbreakable without the book in question.

He'd searched the few volumes Glass had not sold while he and Summer rummaged through the man's study. If the list truly did belong to him, it stood to reason that he would have the book somewhere in his house. Hidden if he was careful. Out in the open if he wasn't.

Considering the amount of port the man drank and the way he played cards, Eliot would have wagered on *not* careful. But all he had found were account ledgers, a book of poetry, and a stack of newspapers.

He'd taken them all. But not one of them was the key to the code. Not unless one of the compromised lady spies was named Raarrzzyx. Which was unlikely.

He rubbed his jaw, frustrated. This was hardly the way to prove he should be working intelligence. Although no one else in the department had cracked the code yet either. Time was running out. He'd suggested treating all of the female spies as compromised and pulling them from the field, and his superior had turned such a bright shade of red he'd nearly suggested the color for Aunt Georgie's parlor walls. The ladies were not called back. They were too necessary, too helpful to the cause. Worth the sacrifice.

It made his stomach burn.

Worse, when Summer might now be part of that sacrifice. Fire turned to acid in his gut.

If Glass was behind everything, he needed to be caught out faster. And if he weren't behind it, they were fucked. The other suspects seemed less and less likely to fit the parameters.

Not to mention, he'd much prefer to crawl into Summer's bed and lick her until she screamed his name. Again. He would never get tired of that. Just the thought of it had him going hard.

The tiny noise from across the hall made him tense in other ways.

He waited until the soft footsteps receded before opening his door and following. It could be a scullery maid come to stoke the fires early, Beatrix or Maggie searching for breakfast. The cat that escaped the kitchens daily to sit in the sun at the top of the grand staircase.

It wasn't.

Of course it wasn't.

It was Summer. He watched her tug her hood over her dark hair and then pull the front door shut behind her.

Cursing, he followed.

MAYFAIR AT DAWN was in disguise, a lady relaxing in her morning gown before the never-ending parade of visitors arrived.

The roads were empty, not yet clogged with the carts of the ragman or deliveries from the markets, and definitely clear of the fashionable carriages carrying the *ton* back home to their beds. It was a place between time, and it seemed to Summer like traveling to another country. The mist was thick around her horses' hooves, echoing the sound of his canter. The air was brisk, the spring dew sparkling on the cobbles and the iron lampposts. Hyde Park was not far, and though generally a haunt for nefarious deeds and illicit duels at this hour of the morning, the Cake House should be safe enough.

Summer rode up to the keeper's house on the north side of the Serpentine. Hyde Park needed caretakers, after all, like anywhere else. And during the summer afternoons, one could stop for syllabub and cheesecakes. For now, the grass lawns sparkled with dew instead of the *ton*. Birds sang in the treetops.

Madeline emerged from a copse of sweet chestnut trees, waving yellow catkins above her head. She looked tired, her hair in a messy twist. "You came."

"Did you think I wouldn't?" Summer dismounted. The curiosity alone would have done her in.

"It's not particularly safe," Madeline pointed out.

It was a test, then, as suspected. "I'm confident my horse can outrun most people. And shouldn't you be across the sea by now?" Summer asked. "If we're speaking of things that are not safe."

Madeline smiled wearily. The lines at the corners of her eyes were more pronounced. "There are things set in motion that must be handled. Goodbyes I need to make."

A lover? Summer didn't ask.

"I'll disappear tomorrow."

"What is in motion?"

She looked Summer up and down, in her fine riding habit, her expensive saddle. The horse that cost more to feed than most people could afford to pay on their own housing. A diamond. *The* Diamond. Summer tried not to let it make her feel inadequate. What a strange turn of events. "Do you really want to know? Because there's always something. There are no holidays in this business," Madeline said. "So you must decide carefully. Is this just a lark?"

Summer grinned. "That was a dreadful pun."

"True. The question holds."

"I want to help," Summer replied simply.

"I imagine a gilded cage is still a cage," Madeline said. "And little birds ought to fly free."

The breeze dipped under the branches, scenting the damp air with Summer's perfume, notes of orange and vanilla and jasmine out of place.

Out of place.

"I *want* to help," she repeated. "If I can." She sighed. "I imagine I do not have the skills," she admitted, though it was like eating raw salt. It would put people in danger to pretend otherwise. "I can't decipher codes. I don't tend to blend into a crowd. Why me?" she asked, because she could not help it.

"Because I know a lark when I see one. I might be *the* Lark, but I am not the *only* one. I have mistresses and harlots, opera singers and flower sellers. But I do not have a *lady*." She sat back. "They'll never see you coming. Even when they look right at you."

Summer tried not to feel a thrill of gratification, and failed.

"And you're very beautiful."

Summer stifled a sigh. "Thank you."

"It's not a compliment," Madeline said. "It's a fact. You have beauty and social standing. You can use them with far more success than most soldiers with a bayonet. I've been looking for someone like you for a very long time." She chuckled. "Blackpool will hate me."

"Blackpool is not my keeper."

"He's the same, you know. A pretty face no one suspects of anything but mirth and merry."

Summer bristled with protectiveness and an absurd need to defend Eliot. Madeline hadn't said anything that wasn't true.

"I have a flock of larks who can blend in anywhere, from church to pawnbroker. What I don't have is a fine lady who can walk through ballrooms and royal drawing rooms like she belongs. We mostly deliver messages hidden in letters, such as the one I sent you. Sometimes in flowers, sometimes in baskets of meat pies at the kitchen door. No one looks twice at us because we are women. They'll look twice at *you*. And we'll use it to our advantage. That is...if you're interested?"

Something very like excitement fluttered in Summer's chest, but it was more than that. Sharp and sweet enough to have her wondering why her eyes suddenly stung. "I'm interested."

"Then take this." Madeline handed Summer a cameo, delicately carved with a bird. Roses circled around, edged with tiny pearls. "For when you need to prove you are not just *Lady Summer*."

Madeline looked pointedly over Summer's shoulder, and she turned to see Eliot waiting on horseback at the top of the hill, all sharp, patient shadows. None of the carefree charm he showed everyone else. Liquid heat softened her thighs when she remembered how they had spent the night. She ought to be far more tired than she was. She only felt exhilarated.

"Your man's here," Madeline murmured.

"He's not my man."

"Isn't he?"

Summer spent the rest of the morning eating crumpets with strawberry jam and sharp cheeses while bouquets of flowers were turned away at the door and sent on to various locations, including flower girls walking the London streets with their baskets. Eliot had escorted her home, sent off a stack of messages, and then left as soon as his battalion of footmen arrived to lurk around the house and look threatening. Aunt Georgie sent them extra crumpets and pink-frosted macarons, greatly decreasing their aura of menace.

They were on their third pot of strong tea with honey in the breakfast room, which was covered in climbing-rose wallpaper and matching dishware. Pink roses danced across plates and teacups, and were painted on the handle of the cutlery. A gold platter piled with pilfered ceramic pineapples sat in the center of the table. Aunt Georgie was very smug about their presence. No one had the heart to tell her that the new earl was unlikely to miss them.

Beatrix looked as proper and tidy as a governess, sipping tea and making notes in her little book. Summer had already written her thank-you notes. Maggie yawned wide enough that Summer could have counted her back teeth. Her hair was caught in a knot of wild curls. What a motley bunch they made. And how at home she suddenly felt, after being unmoored since leaving Cornwall.

"I'll have the Glass guestlist from last night by dinner," Aunt Georgie said. "Just in case you need it."

"By dinner *tonight*?" Beatrix looked up, impressed. "That's rather quick."

"Pish." Aunt Georgie waved that away. "Lady Susan likes to chat. And show off. It will be easy as pie." She sniffed. "Summer, I do hope your mother isn't there."

"I might also be able to get a list of the servants," Beatrix added. "But it's not likely to be complete. I am quite certain she hired help for the evening. And that's not to mention the flower services, the musicians, the deliveries."

"I'll tell her I'm hosting my own event," Aunt Georgie said. "And I'll ask her advice. I'll know the names of the mice in the attic by the time soup is served." She giggled. Summer hadn't heard her make such a silly, joyful sound in months. Something unclenched in her chest. "This is fun," Aunt Georgie continued. "I feel like a real spy. But I will leave you to the rest of your puzzles." She bustled away on her mission, calling for her bonnet and her gloves. The ones embroidered with begonias. She only wore those when she was at war. She wore them rather a lot when Summer's mother was in town, it had to be said.

"How many footmen will follow her, do you think?" Beatrix asked without looking up.

"At least three," Summer replied. "Two at minimum. And I'm not convinced Eliot realizes we've noticed they are ra-ther...violent looking for footmen."

"Eliot, is it?" Maggie grinned, adding an obscene amount of sugar to her tea. Beatrix muttered something about the state of her teeth. Maggie ignored her. "I thought you hoity-toities only used titles."

"He's been irritating me since we were children," Summer pointed out. "I've more than earned the right."

"Is that so?" Maggie asked, tongue firmly planted in cheek. "And here I thought it was because I wasn't the only one sneaking up the stairs last night trying not to wake the household."

Summer tried very hard not to smile. "I'm sure I don't know what you mean."

"I was coming in from a show at Astley's," Maggie persisted. "What were *you* doing, I wonder?"

"Keep wondering."

"The earl," Beatrix said.

"Pardon?"

"She was doing the earl," Beatrix elaborated. Summer choked on a bite of crumpet. Beatrix only smiled. "She did ask."

Maggie chortled into her cup. "He's handsome enough, and gossip has it he knows what he's doing."

"There's gossip about him in East London?"

"We're poor, Summer. We're not blind." She raised her eyebrows expectantly. "Well?"

"Well what?" Summer tried to look innocent, failed dismally and dissolved into a laugh. "I will only say he is not...disappointing."

Maggie sighed. "I definitely need more details."

He was deeply distracting, with clever fingers and eyes that saw everything.

"We have a traitor to foil," Summer reminded her instead.

"I ride a horse while balancing on my hands. I'm very good at doing two things at once."

Summer stood up. "I have to go. I need to sneak out the back while the footmen are busy with Aunt Georgie. I mean to get my hands on Glass's art collection today, and they might spook him."

"I want to know more about what you got your hands on last night."

Summer chucked her napkin at Maggie. "You are terrible."

"Eastenders are just more fun, Lady Summer." She cackled at Summer's back. "Haven't you figured that out already?"

THE GLASS TOWNHOUSE was still filled with yellow roses, now starting to wilt, but the detritus of abandoned glasses and plates and half-finished desserts had already been carted to the kitchens for cleaning. Maidservants swarmed like bees, sweeping, dusting, polishing. The butler led Summer to the main drawing room, where several gentlemen far too old to be reasonable suitors sat around Lady April, mostly ignoring her. Three of them had proposed to Summer the years she came out, and they were too old for *her* then. Lord Tottenham drank whiskey in the corner and scowled at them.

"Lady Summer Winter," the butler announced.

Why her mother, who had never known a moment of whimsy in her life, had chosen to name her daughter Summer with the last name of Winter, she would never know. Perhaps it was to induce her to marry as soon as possible, that she might change it. Summer wouldn't put it past her. Callum had one destiny: to be duke. And it was everything. But Summer had a destiny too, to marry well for the glory of the family name, and do so quickly and with as little fuss as possible.

Obviously, Summer had not obeyed.

The conversation paused, and assessing glances were sent in Summer's direction. She smiled at April, who leapt to her feet and curtsied, looking like she might weep in relief. "Lady Summer!"

Summer drew closer. "Gentlemen," she said pleasantly when they rose politely. "Thank you so much for keeping young Lady April company. I'm afraid I am going to be very greedy and claim her for myself now." Her smile did not falter when they blinked at her. She motioned to the butler, who hurried forward with hats and gloves. "Do have a lovely day."

They followed the butler out meekly, mostly because they didn't know what else to do.

Lord Tottenham laughed. Loudly. They surely heard him. "I didn't know I could just boot them out."

"You can't." Summer smiled, curtsying. "But *I* can."

"Then you must teach my granddaughter everything you know. Lady Susan was not available as chaperone today—she was wrung out, I'm afraid." And about to deal with the full force of Aunt Georgie. Summer hoped Lady Susan had a good headache powder on hand.

"Oh, but I could never ask a room full of gentlemen to *leave!*" But there was a gleam in April's eye that Summer recognized and approved of.

"We have very few arenas of battle afforded to us," Summer said. She remembered being seventeen. Trading the strictures of the schoolroom for the equally random strictures of the Season. More than two dances with the same gentleman was shocking enough to presume an engagement had already been made. Wearing red might spark unkind rumors. No obvious lip salve, but don't appear too sallow, either. Plentiful cleavage, but not too much cleavage. Encourage, but don't outright flirt.

"The drawing room is one of those arenas. Don't give quarter, Lady April. For they never will." She paused. "Or have I overstepped? Did you wish to marry a man three times your age?"

"No!" Lady April shuddered. She lowered her voice. "Why does Lord Wosley smell like leeks?"

"Old men often have trouble with their teeth and eat a lot of potage and soups."

"Hey now," her grandfather protested amiably. He clacked his jaws together like castanets. "I have all my own teeth, and I don't smell like stewed vegetables."

"Of course not," Summer agreed. "You are quite above and beyond their like."

Lord Tottenham sent April a wry look. "And that, my dear, is flattery. You'll learn that trick as well."

Summer laughed and looped her arm through his. "Lord Tottenham, you promised me an exclusive art tour so that I might gloat to my friends. And as a gentleman with strong teeth who smells only of very good cologne, I must assume you keep your word."

He smiled down at her. "It would be a pleasure, my dear." He held out his other arm to April. "Shall we?"

Lord Tottenham led them to the blue parlor, the doors now unlocked and opened wide. The ceiling was painted like the sky, and all of the cushions were velvet the shade of cornflowers. Dust motes danced like fairy lights. The empty places on shelves and on the walls were obvious. There were far more of them than accounted for the art contained in open crates along the window. He had already sold off everything he could sell. Rumors of his insolvency appeared to be true. Interesting.

Summer kept her expression neutral even as she wanted to pounce on everything in the boxes and shake them like rattles to see if anything fell out. Lord Tottenham watched her as they approached, and she adjusted her smile.

"I apologize for the lack of presentation, Lady Summer," he said. "I'm afraid they are being delivered just as soon as we are done here."

"Then I am truly honored," she said. "You really have given me something to gloat about."

"Won't your friends see it all at the gala?" April asked.

"Those who will attend, yes. But novelty is very rare in Mayfair, and everyone wants to be special." Summer peered into the boxes, wondering how she might better inspect everything. "And as my circle consider themselves art aficionados, this will be quite a coup for me."

Lady Ophelia couldn't care less about art. Haywood only wanted to know if someone would paint his portrait, even though she had painted it for him three different times. And Maggie and Beatrix would laugh at being referred to as afficionados. Her new friends were not the type to be impressed. And Eliot was also too accustomed to his aunt's peculiar taste to be impressed.

Was he considered a friend? A lover? Both? He'd been a thorn in her side for so long that she scarcely knew anymore. Could he be all three?

"This is a lovely piece." Summer skimmed her fingertips over a vase, very like her fish-man. *Promising.* "Roman, isn't it? May I?"

Lord Tottenham nodded, and she lifted it carefully free of its protective nest of cloth. It was curved and elegant, with nary a fish-man.

In other words, boring.

She took a surreptitious peek down the neck, but there was only darkness. Nothing rattled when she turned it around to look at the other side. "Beautiful."

"You know your art, Lady Summer," Lord Tottenham said. "I admit, I find it not worth the fuss. All these galas and exhibits for old junk. For all we know, they used that vase as a spittoon. I'd rather have a portrait of my best girl here."

She had to laugh. "I suppose that's true. But I've always loved any kind of art. The colors, the way it speaks without words." To April she added, "And it is helpful to have a particular interest, especially during your first Season. It gives you something to fill the silences with and also makes you memorable, if that is your wish. More importantly, it gives you something else to think about, which is even better."

April hesitated. "I like stories of Joan of Arc. And turtles."

"Very memorable. They will decide who you are—if they have not already. But you don't have to let them."

Lord Tottenham waved to the footman, who appeared in the doorway. "There you are. Come and show Lady Summer some of these pieces, would you? And be careful."

The footman bowed and hurried to comply. He lifted out three more vases, a small painting of a shipwreck, and three Roman busts, only one of which retained a nose.

Not a single helpful clue fell out at her feet.

She was a bit vexed over it, actually.

"There are three more paintings," Lord Tottenham said. "Great, big, ugly things, but they were already loaned out to the Royal Academy of Art at Somerset House."

"A shame, but I'm so grateful to have seen this part of the collection. Thank you, Lord Tottenham."

He and his granddaughter escorted her back to the foyer, leaving her no opportunity to come up with a reason that might situate her near Lord Glass's bedroom. If there was no incriminating evidence in his study or his art collection, surely there might be something there?

She said her farewells, collected her gloves from the butler, and stepped out into the bright sunshine.

Where Eliot waited for her on the front step, expression hard.

Chapter Eighteen

"YOU'RE SCOWLING, LORD Blackpool." She beamed at him.

"And that makes you happy?" His scowl did not budge.

She shrugged one shoulder. "You smile at everyone else. That scowl, I flatter myself, is just for me."

"It is," he muttered. He added a glower down the length of his nose. "You didn't wait for me."

"You left without *me* first, I must point out." He grumbled at that. She raised her eyebrows. "Were you successful in your endeavors?"

"I'm afraid not."

"And it's made you peevish."

"I am not peevish," he said evenly before leaning closer. He nipped her earlobe, right there in public, on the front step of a Mayfair townhouse where anyone might see them. Carriages rolled by. Pedestrians walked along the sidewalk in bonnets and crowned hats. The unexpectedness of the nip sent a bolt of heat straight to her quim. Her thighs actually trembled. From a little scrape of his teeth.

And then he straightened. And just like that, he was Lord Blackpool again.

"Now who's teasing?" she muttered.

"I'm not the one who smells like oranges."

"My perfume is hardly teasing you."

"Isn't it?" He offered her his arm, and she took it, trying to corral her disordered wits. Memories of what he had done to her body, of what she had done to his, rushed through her. She wanted to do it all again. And again.

She halted suddenly. "Where's my carriage?"

The one waiting for them was polished and painted with the Blackpool family crest.

"I sent it home."

"Presumptuous."

"Necessary." He tipped his hat to a group of ladies passing by, one of whom sighed audibly. Summer knew exactly how she felt. *Damn it.* "You left without me *and* without a footman, I might add."

"It's the middle of the afternoon. And no one is likely to think the Diamond is hunting a traitor."

"Did you forget you were held at pistol point?" he nearly shouted, his composure cracking.

What did it say about her that she had, possibly, forgotten that? Just a little. So much had happened since then, not the least of which had left her body aching in all the right places. She preferred to hold on to those memories.

Eliot, it seemed, was perfectly capable of holding on to both.

And what else did it say about her that the obvious slip of his calculated poise made her feel even warmer all over? Something funny happened behind her ribcage.

"I didn't mean to worry you," she said. "But I'm not trailing an army of footmen behind me, especially when they look better suited to the boxing ring. It's hardly subtle. The aim is *not* to spook Lord Glass, if you'll recall. I don't know why I keep having to remind you of that."

"My head exploding is also hardly subtle," he pointed out. "Please get in the carriage. I don't like you anywhere near Glass."

"He's not at home. I will get in your carriage, but only because, as it happens, I have information." She tilted her head, grinning. "Admit it, you're impressed again."

"Get in the carriage, Summer, before I throw you over my shoulder."

She paused at that image.

He groaned. Audibly. "I am begging you."

She slid onto the seat, smiling primly. After all, he'd made her beg just last night. "Now, was that so hard?"

He sat across from her, smiling wryly in return. "Very hard, actually."

She caught her lower lip between her teeth. His gaze dropped to the movement.

"What did I say would happen if you insisted on teasing me?"

She had the sudden urge to fan herself. Why was it so hot? It was never this hot in London.

"Summer?" he said softly. "Answer me."

"Consequences." Was that her voice? Breathless and yearning?

"That's right. Remember that later, when I get you properly alone and all to myself."

As threats went, this one was her favorite.

"We need to go to Somerset House," she said, before she could suggest something much more outrageous. And far more enjoyable.

Eliot thumped on the roof and relayed the destination to his driver. The horses pulled away from the curb, and the carriage swayed gently. The curtains were gray velvet and the ceiling above painted with a stormy sky instead of the usual cherubs and roses. Lightning glowed at the edges, painted in the most interesting shades of white and yellow. Unexpected. Just like Eliot.

"Glass is definitely up to his neck in shady dealings," he said. "Though nothing I can confidently link to the Mayfair Art Collectors or the spy list."

"Yet."

"Yet."

"I was able to see most of this collection, if not as closely as I would have liked."

"And?"

"A safe and somewhat boring collection; nowhere near as interesting as your aunt's."

"A riot in a paint factory would not be as interesting."

"True. At any rate, I couldn't find anything hidden inside any of the pieces. I was hoping for a full confession."

He growled. Just a little. "That was a risk."

"A tiny one," she allowed. "Barely worth mentioning."

"I heartily disagree."

"You usually do." London bustled outside the window as they made their way toward the Strand. It wouldn't take very long at this time of day. "He also has three paintings which are hanging at the academy at the moment."

"And you fancy a look."

"Yes. Not to mention that there is always a Collector hanging about the Academy, wanting to talk about the merit of his collection."

"It's worth a shot," Eliot agreed. "But not worth putting you in danger."

That warmth again, that he cared. That whatever else this confusing heat between them might be, he cared. It was nice.

Also bothersome. Because she liked it so much. Too much.

"I've got you, don't I?" she asked archly. "A spy of my very own."

"Yes," he said firmly, almost like a warning. "You do."

He reached out and tugged on her wrists, drawing her to the edge of the seat. His mouth closed over hers, a slow, deep kiss meant to drug her out of asking too many questions. He licked at her decadently, before sucking on her lower lip, just once. His teeth followed, scraping gently. She gasped before she could stop herself. It was too easy for him to take control of her body, to make it sing.

"You won this hand, plum," he said against her mouth as the

carriage pulled to a stop in front of Somerset House. "Don't get used to it."

She nipped back because it gave her pleasure. Gave *them* pleasure.

"Too late."

SOMERSET HOUSE WAS an enormous white-gray building with a row of columns standing guard over several archways. Behind it, the Thames teemed with boats and the work of the major thoroughfare of the city. The façade faced the Strand, with the church of St. Mary-Le-Strand to the side. Summer and Eliot crossed into the massive courtyard, bordered by the wings of London's first public buildings. The Stamp Office and the Tax Office occupied part of the structure, and the Royal Academy of the Arts occupied the north wing.

They promenaded toward the gallery, like any other couple. It was always busy, but at least was not a complete crush with the Summer Exhibition not yet hung. Families moved through the cavernous room, dwarfed by a truly dizzying array of paintings. They fit like puzzle pieces from chair rail to ceiling. Those at the very top were tilted down to avoid the glare of light. If Glass's paintings were up there, they'd never get any secret information.

A woman stood in front of a painting of the Graces, cradling a small poodle with ribbons looped around its collar. He lifted his lips off his teeth, clearly not appreciative of the art. "Don't be so grumpy," the woman scolded him. "Those are not the manners of a gentleman, Aristotle."

Summer allowed herself to get lost for just a moment, in the sheer volume of art surrounding her. Of the thought that she might have taken lessons at the Academy, were she Callum. Or Eliot. Or any man with talent, for that matter.

Eliot followed her gaze to a bucolic landscape. "I like your forgery better," he whispered. "Much more spirit."

"I copied a painting with very little spirit."

"Your version had it. You just need to know how to look."

She liked him a little more every time he opened his mouth.

That was going to be a problem.

Not today. Today was for espionage and appreciating art. Not that she expected to find Lord Glass sharing his plots in a villainous whisper worthy of the stage, but at the very least she could confirm whether his paintings actually belonged to Aunt Georgie.

They did not.

Two were of racehorses and another was a landscape of a ruined abbey. Pretty enough, but hardly original. Definitely not something Aunt Georgie collected.

"You're frowning," Eliot pointed out as she craned her neck back to study them. She was gratified that they had been skied by being set well above the prime display line. Served him right.

"I do not like those paintings," she said.

"They are rather bland for your taste. I know how you feel about fish-men."

"Exactly," she said. It nagged at her, but she could not say why. "Aside from the fish-man and that happy horror of the horse outside his study, Glass's collection is quite unremarkable."

"And this bothers you?"

"Aesthetically, yes," she muttered. "But mostly, I wonder why. Why *those* pieces?"

"Sometimes it's coincidence," he replied. "Everything feels like it should connect dots in this type of work, but sometimes it just...doesn't."

"Hmm."

They took another turn around the gallery. The woman with the dog tried to get him to stop eating another woman's feathered bonnet. By the shriek, she was unsuccessful.

Outside, they waited for Blackpool's carriage to pull back around, as the coachman had to drive around the block due to the building traffic. Londoners hurried to and fro on errands, or else lingered in the courtyard, enjoying the sunshine. Placard men milled about advertising soap and boot polish. Costermongers shouted their wares, from lemons and oranges to nutmeg graters and painted bonnet boxes.

"Sweet violets, penny a bunch!" a young girl called out, weaving through the crowds. She carried a large basket that threatened to overbalance her. Violets and bunches of watercress made a little thicket inside, like the forest floor. "Watercress!" She spotted Summer, her wide eyes darting to the cameo she wore. "Roses for sale!"

As Summer bent her head to inspect the nosegays, the girl turned her basket slightly, showing a rough drawing of a bird in a circle of roses. The very same as her cameo. She stilled, expectation sharpening in her chest. Was she truly a spy now?

"Roses for you, your ladyship." The girl handed her the nosegay, and Eliot handed her money.

"And here I thought you'd have me buy you diamonds," he said.

"I prefer chocolate." She always had, but her mother worried about her figure and the state of her teeth and had turned away every suitor who carried sweets from the very first. Diamonds were *ducal*.

"Noted."

The nosegay was mostly violets, with a single red rose in the center. Tucked in among the stalks tied with twine was a charm in the shape of the bird. She didn't know which part of the nosegay was the message, or if it was a combination thereof.

"Twenty-three Bruton Street," the girl whispered. "Leave your nosegay in the ladies' retiring room."

And then she was off, scampering away, shouting her wares like any other street seller. Her feet were bare and dirty.

"I hope you overpaid," Summer said.

"I paid less for the chandelier in my front hall," Eliot assured her. "And I let her pick my pocket." He nudged her toward the carriage as it pulled into a very narrow space, causing several shouts. "Take your secret message and let's get off the streets."

She widened her eyes at him. "How did you know?"

"I know what your cameo means, and I saw inside her basket. And I know how the Lark operates." He did not look thrilled. Or sound it. His jaw was clenched, the slash of his eyebrows tightening to dig a line between them.

"At least the day was not a complete waste of my time," she said cheerfully.

He glanced down at her, and there was enough brewing in his dark eyes to make her attempt a conciliatory smile. "A waste of your time?" he echoed. "Your concern is that if you were not put in even more danger, you would have *wasted your time?*"

"Yes, of course."

He made a sound halfway between a growl and snarl caught inside a sigh before pulling the door open for her.

"Get in."

Chapter Nineteen

ELIOT FOLLOWED, AFTER murmuring something to the driver. As she settled herself comfortably, the horses pulled into a walk. Did she know who lived at Twenty-three Bruton Street? She could not recall. She'd attended balls and dinners and card parties all through Mayfair, up and down every street. She would go through her invitations as soon as she got home. Or ask Aunt Georgie.

"Be careful, Summer. Madeline is slippery. She does not care for the English any more than she cares for the French, despite her work. She just happens to live here. Her mother was French and her father English."

"I know."

"You know? How?"

"She told me."

"She *told* you?"

"Are you going to repeat everything I say?" She tucked the nosegay carefully into her reticule, making sure not to crush the petals.

"If I do, will I understand you any better?" He was grumbling, and she paid it no mind. She was coming to realize that he understood her better than anyone. He saw her. Actually saw *her*. It was not a discovery she had expected.

But then, neither was becoming a spy.

They turned left, the traffic a blur of colors and sounds through the window. "We're going the wrong way," she said.

Eliot pulled the curtain closed. "We're going the long way around."

She turned to him. "We are? Why?"

"I need the extra time."

Something stirred awake in her lower belly at the tone of his voice. "For what?"

"Didn't we agree you broke the rules?" he asked softly. "Visiting the Glass house without protection? Teasing me?"

"Not my rules," she shot back. "Yours."

His face went stern again, though he smiled a half-smile she had never seen before. It was amused, sharp. Nearly predatory. A frisson of trepidation touched her before he did.

And she liked it.

Very much.

Anticipation and desire immediately flooded through her.

"There are consequences." He yanked her forward along the seat. "*Lady* Summer."

"I—" She didn't know what she had planned to say, only that pushing and teasing Eliot had always been the standard.

Seldom with such delicious *consequences*. If he wanted to call them that.

"I thought you were going to wait until we were properly alone."

"I decided I couldn't wait a moment longer," he growled.

He still hadn't kissed her, but he held her so firmly, so close, that the words died in her throat regardless. She was too busy trying not to pant. She felt electrified. Waiting for something, something she knew she desperately wanted, even if she had no idea what that was. Yet. Her entire body strained toward him even as she stayed still as a doe in the woods.

"What do you think I should do to you?" he asked.

"I have a few ideas," she breathed.

He laughed, and it was soft, and it was dangerous.

And it was perfect.

He gripped her chin, tilting her head back. He searched her eyes, clearly approving of what he saw. His fingers tightened. "Are you tired of getting away with everything?"

"Certainty not."

"Let's see, shall we?" he murmured in her ear, raising goose-bumps along her neck and down her spine. She leaned forward, trying to touch any part of him. "Ah, ah," he scolded, his knees spread between hers, opening her thighs but also effectively pinning her in place. "You're not making the decision here, plum." He dragged open-mouthed kisses down her jaw, licking into her clavicle. She shivered. Who knew the clavicle was directly connected to her nipples? They pebbled, straining to be touched, to be licked. "Who's making the decisions?" he demanded.

She bit her lower lip. She knew if she could just reach him, she could tease him into giving them both what they wanted without her ever having to make such an admission. Except he held her wrists now, both of them, secured to the cushion on either side of her. Her thighs went soft, held open, waiting. "Eliot."

"I asked you a question," he said with that unwavering ruth-lessness that spoke straight to her quim. She was swelling, dripping. And he was still so far away.

"You," she finally murmured.

"What was that?"

She narrowed her eyes. "I was going to say that *you* make the decisions, but you don't seem to have the ballocks—"

He growled, pulling her over his lap so she straddled him. It was sudden, and he took all of her weight. Her dress bunched around her knees. His cock pressed against her warmth, hard. She moaned. "Little devil," he said, the tendons of his neck working. "Trying to push me, are you?"

She rubbed against him in reply.

He reared up and pulled her neckline down with his teeth,

pulling at the edge of her stays until her breast was finally in his mouth. He sucked her nipple in long, hot pulls until she fell forward, gasping. Bolts of pure pleasure shot down to her quim, throbbing through her bud. When she made sounds in the back of her throat, he only moved to her other breast.

She shifted restlessly against his patience. *"Eliot."*

"I don't think you're wet enough, plum."

He stroked between her folds, soft and wet and eager. She whimpered.

"Not yet."

She'd never been so wet in her life. So desperate. She fumbled for the fall of his breeches and grabbed her wrists. "Hands up," he ordered her, guiding them to the ceiling. "If you disobey, I stop touching you."

She called him names. He grinned as if she'd recited a poem about the color of his eyes.

The bastard.

And then he was stroking through her warmth, circling her bud, sliding a finger inside her, followed by another. He pumped in and out, and she clenched around him. She dropped one of her hands, wanting to touch him, to make him as wild as he was making her.

He stilled.

She nearly shouted.

"What did I say?" he asked calmly, as if the carriage wasn't rocking her into his hardness. He held her hips, denying her. She choked, flattening her palm to the ceiling again. "Good girl."

The reward was instantaneous. For all that he was teasing her, he was teasing himself too.

Not anymore.

His fingers moved over her, inside her, slick with her desire and clever with his. A soft glide over her bud, a circle, a flick of his thumb. Again and again in a pattern that threatened to pull her apart. She rubbed against him, gasping as the hot tingle of her climax gathered in her thighs, rose higher, engulfed her. She spasmed and shivered, consumed.

And then he reared up, filling her completely.

Finally. *Finally.*

"Again," he demanded. "Come on my cock, plum."

The carriage rocked with them, rattling over the crack in the road, pulling to sudden stops, rolling again. It added to the rhythm. Summer felt herself getting wetter and wetter as Eliot plunged into her. She tried to meet each thrust, but her hands were still pressed up above her head. He took her hips again, bringing her down over his length until she was so full that she could only clench helplessly around him. He came with a groan, and she followed.

She slumped over him, catching her breath. "Were you trying to teach me a lesson?" she asked.

"I was."

She grinned, shivering with an unexpected aftershock of pleasure. "I'm a very slow learner."

He kissed her slowly, deeply, eyes hooded. "Thank God for that."

As it turned out, Lord and Lady Bathurst lived at Twenty-three Bruton Street, and they were having a party. To which Summer was invited.

Eliot was not.

She might have crowed about it. Just a bit.

A lot.

Not that it mattered. Doors did not shut in the Earl of Blackpool's face. They never had, and she imagined they never would. The butler at the party would not even consider asking for his invitation.

As she accepted her cloak from Thistle, Eliot came down the stairs. "Change of plans," he said.

She adjusted the ribbon. "Oh?"

"I've been called to meet with my supervisor at the War Office."

"I am sure the many ladies will struggle to survive without you." She herself felt a pang of disappointment, which she promised herself she would murder with a plate of chocolate biscuits at the first opportunity. Lady Bathurst was a known connoisseur of sweets, and there was bound to be an excellent selection between dance sets.

Eliot approached her slowly, every step a hint, a promise. A dare.

She narrowed her eyes immediately. "What is it?"

"Will you wait for me?"

"You could be hours. You can meet me there."

"I don't like you running errands for the Lark alone. It isn't safe."

"For the Crown, not just for the Lark," she pointed out.

He snorted. "That is not any safer, I assure you."

"And I'm not alone. I have Tom." He frowned. She rolled her eyes. "The footman you hired to follow me about at these events."

He arched a brow. "Oh, him."

"Yes, him. So, you see, I'll be perfectly fine."

His gaze raked over her. "You *are* perfect."

Because she felt a little bit perfect when he looked at her that way, she poked him in the chest. Hard. "We agreed on no empty flattery."

"Did we?" His voice dropped, grew husky.

"I know what you're doing." She *felt* what he was doing. *Everywhere.*

"Is it working?"

She sniffed, but goosebumps had already snuck up her neck, across her collarbones.

He smiled, following them. "That is some comfort." He nipped her earlobe. "You'll miss me, won't you, plum? We could have such a better night if we stayed home."

Thistle had abandoned them, and the footmen were in the dining room, attending to Aunt Georgie and her supper. There was no one to see them. It was a risk, of course, but tonight was for risks, wasn't it? She closed the last bit of distance between them, catching him by surprise. His back hit the wall, and his expression was amused. Amused until she reached down, and then it went just a little bit feral. She nearly moaned. He moaned first as she closed her hand around his hard length, dragging up, then down.

A tiny noise down the hall had her stepping away, cheeks flushed.

"You'll pay for that later," he rasped.

"Promise?" she taunted him.

Those stern, dark eyes, the clenching in his jaw. The coiled energy in every line of his body. All so delicious. "I do, in point of fact."

If her breath trembled when she released it, at least his did as well.

"I'll make a deal with you," she said. "When you return, you'll tell me why you were called to the War Office on such short notice, and when *I* return, I shall tell you how my delivery went."

"That's not a deal," he pointed out. "That is simply you getting your own way."

She grinned. "I could instead *not* tell you where I go or what I find out."

He blanched. He actually blanched. *"No."*

"Then we have ourselves an accord."

"It's like haggling with the fishwives down at the docks."

She beamed. "That's the nicest thing you've ever said to me." One of the nicest things anyone had ever said to her, actually.

"Just this morning I told you that you were as beautiful as the evening star."

"Bah."

"Poetry gets a bah. But accusing you of being cunning is likely to make you swoon."

"You ought to remember that."

"I am unlikely to forget," he promised in a little growl in her ear.

They broke apart again when Thistle returned with Eliot's hat. They stepped out into the busy Mayfair night together but broke away on the sidewalk. "Eliot?" she murmured before climbing into the waiting carriage. It belonged to Aunt Georgie, so naturally it was bright yellow and adorned with the most ostentatious pineapples.

"Yes, plum?"

"Don't let them put you in a little box," she said. "You can be a code breaker. There's no one better suited. Well, maybe Beatrix."

His lips twitched. "You are not wrong."

"You're not just a rake, you know."

"And you're not just a duke's daughter."

They smiled at each other, small, hesitant smiles.

"Eliot?"

"Yes?"

"Why do you call me plum?"

"Maybe one day I'll tell you. We can wager for it."

Eliot watched her carriage pull away until she was out of sight. She knew because she watched him back.

ELIOT WENT STRAIGHT back to Lord Glass's townhouse after a fruitless meeting with the War Office. They did not want to hear his thoughts on the cipher or the safety of the larks.

They wanted him to seduce the wife of the ambassador of Vienna.

The thought made him want to put his fist through the wall of his carriage, where Summer had ridden him until they both came apart. The ambassador's wife did not stand a chance. He could charm her, dance until dawn, whisper compliments, but he had no desire to put his mouth on anyone but Summer.

His commanding officer did not care. Sweet nothings, not ciphers. It was an order.

As he was an earl, Eliot did not often take orders. He had no intention of starting now. He would break that code. Somehow. Summer, for some reason, believed in him. It made him feel like he could take on Napoleon's army himself.

But first, Lord Glass.

He was teetering on the edge of several bad decisions—anyone with eyes could see it. Eliot intended for him to make those mistakes in a way that led him to the code.

Time to call in his debt.

He'd pay Glass a visit. Storm into his house in a lather over debts owed and a gentleman's honor, all while he was dressing for the evening's festivities. He'd have a better chance of locating any books Glass might be keeping by his bed.

No time like the present.

The butler greeted him at the door, informing him that Lord Glass was still above stairs.

Perfect.

"No need to announce me." Eliot tossed his hat onto a table and took the stairs two at a time, with the butler sputtering behind him.

A footman met him at the top of stairs. "My lord?"

"Glass's bedroom."

"If you would—"

"Glass's bedroom, or I start opening doors at random."

"Third on the left," he blurted out.

"Good man."

Eliot shoved open the door without knocking. Glass stood in front of his looking glass while his valet emerged from the dressing room with a freshly starched cravat. They both froze when Eliot leaned in the doorway. "I'm here for my money, Glass."

Through the mirror, there was a flash of panic in Glass's eyes, but when he turned to face Eliot, he was smiling. "Bursting into a man's bedroom isn't the thing, old man."

Eliot straightened. "You owe me six thousand pounds, *old*

man."

The valet looked disgusted before fixing on the mask of all trained valets across London: polite, haughty, and entirely deaf and blind to the dealings of their employer.

Eliot noted the half-packed trunks. "You're not running out on me, are you? The Season's just begun."

"Of course not." Glass drained his glass of port.

There were a few books on the floor by his bed, more on the table by the fire. Not much else. He'd been selling things in earnest since Eliot and Summer broke into his study. Definitely motive. Possibly helpful, as well. He'd keep anything needed for his code.

"Where's my blunt?" Eliot pushed. Glass was already sweating. He didn't think it was a direct result of his intimidation. The man seemed to be in a constant state of dampness. Panic did that to a person. "I'd hate to have to tell the *ton* how you don't come up to scratch. Hard to find someone willing to trust your word when it comes to your daughter's dowry."

Glass visibly paled. Eliot thought, with some disgust, that if he pushed much further, the man would collapse and be of no use whatsoever. He was unraveling. It did not bode well for the list of names he held hostage.

Eliot bit back a curse. Best to make this quick.

He strode forward, using his height to loom. Summer would have poked fun at him for it. The valet took three giant steps backward. "I'll take collateral. For now." He glanced around. "You don't have much, Glass. It's not reassuring." He gathered the books by the bed, on the table painted with gold ivy leaves.

Glass sputtered. "But…"

"I'm not particularly in the mood for a duel at dawn. It's frightfully early, and the dew will ruin my boots," Eliot drawled.

Glass poured more port. "Of course not, of course not," he babbled. His mouth was already stained.

Satisfied, Eliot stormed out. Lady April squeaked, startled by the earl roaming the halls like a runaway bull. "Lord Blackpool!"

"Lady April."

Lord Tottenham emerged further down the hall. "Blackpool, what the hell are you doing here?"

"Business."

"Stealing books is business?"

Eliot smiled. "Collateral. Not much else left here, is there?"

"Oh." This from April, who held a copy of *Debrett's* in her hand. She handed it over hesitantly.

"He doesn't want that," Tottenham boomed, his whiskers quivering with outrage. "You need it, don't you, ferret? How else is she to learn about any future prospects for a husband?" He scowled at Eliot. "Don't punish my granddaughter for her father's debts."

Eliot didn't reply. He had no intention of troubling the young Lady April. And every household boasted a copy of *Debrett's*. He'd already checked it for the cipher, having seen it in Glass's study the night of the ball.

Eliot smiled at April, who looked ready to chuck the book at his head and dive under the nearest bed. "Keep it."

"Thank you, Lord Blackpool."

Outside, Eliot paid a hackney driver an obscene amount of money to hand over the reins. He waited for Glass to emerge and then followed him to his club, and two gaming hells.

It was spectacularly unhelpful.

And it niggled at him, like a puzzle missing a piece.

Chapter Twenty

T HE BATHURST BALL was not particularly interesting. Candles dripped from the ceiling, crystal gleamed, music swelled. Dancers danced. Jewels glittered. There were sly glances, covert touches. All the things Summer knew as well as she knew her own name. But there was also a truly spectacular assortment of sweets, which was a balm.

And she had a secret mission that was the best sweet of all.

It even made up for her mother being in attendance, already sniffing disdainfully at Summer's dancing slippers with the red ribbons. Spies for the Crown did not fret over their mothers. Women who worked for the infamous Lark did not falter.

Truly, her mother had not made her falter in years, but her stomach always dropped just a little, until it caught up with her head. She and her mother were too different, as were the things they wanted. For one, Summer was not a boy. She was not an heir to the dukedom, and so she should serve it blindly in penance. Thankfully, her brother had never felt that way. Indeed, he had always protected her. He never snitched on her wilder plots, and she never let him go very long without dragging him into one of those same plots. He had needed more laughter, even as a child. Especially as a child. The day she heard Cat make him laugh, long before they married, was the day Summer decided Cat would be her sister-in-law.

And now, finally, she was at a ball like the hundreds she had attended before, but she was decidedly *not* bored. Ennui didn't threaten to drown her. She did not feel invisible in that itchy way that came with being looked at.

No one here noticed anything different, but she knew the truth. They saw a woman who floated from distraction to distraction, a crowning glory for every host and hostess. But it did not sting the way it had begun to over the last few years.

When someone asked her to dance, she accepted with a smile. If she barreled toward the ladies' retiring room as soon as she arrived, it would look odd. Or as if she had eaten bad fish for nuncheon. She was Lady Summer, and the title, the constricting life it came with, was suddenly sharp as a sword. And this time it was not pointed at her. It was *her* weapon to wield.

If only Eliot were here with her.

That was a sobering thought. How much she wanted him nearby. How she could not help but search the crowd for him. How intrinsic he had become to her day. And her nights.

She brought her attention back to the dance, flashing her smile like a calling card. Four more gentlemen begged to write their names on her dance card the moment the music faded. She accepted and did not even feel resentful about it. She used to love to dance when she first came out. It was nearly as bracing as running, which she was not allowed to do as a young lady. Nor as an older lady, but the fields of Cornwall never told her secrets. But in London, dancing would have to do.

She was very aware of the tiny nosegay in her reticule. It sat next to her cameo of a bird in a circle of roses. She understood Aunt Georgie a little better too. The cameo was just a thing, an item. But it represented so much more. It was already heavy with her stories, her hopes.

She danced for another hour until she begged off to refresh herself with a glass of lemonade.

And a trip to the ladies' retiring room.

She waited until the last dance before the food was brought

out, when she knew it would be busiest. Everyone wanted to make sure their hair stayed pinned and their cheeks glowed when they went into supper, hopefully on the arm of a very handsome and very eligible lord.

Lady Bathurst's private morning room had been converted for the evening, and it was packed. Even with the windows open, the air was too hot. Mirrors were scattered about like shards of ice after a snowstorm. Chamber pots stood behind screens, and lady's maids waited with sewing supplies and hair tongs. All for the secret business of floating around the ballroom like someone out of a painting, like something utterly unreal.

The mix of perfumes and hair tonics made Summer cough. It was awful.

And tonight, she loved it.

"Lady Summer, would you care for champagne?" Lady Bathurst asked.

Summer found, for the first time, that she would rather drink gin then another glass of clear, glittering champagne from a crystal flute.

"It's French," Lady Bathurst confessed. "I don't see how depriving ourselves of fine food and wine will help the war, do you?"

"Indeed not," Summer said, accepting a glass. She took a tiny sip and then set it down. There was no bird in a circle of roses anywhere on Lady Bathurst's person. She might be a very good actress, but Summer thought probably her morning room was a relay point, not a destination. Although, if she drank smuggled champagne, someone in the household had connections. Still, she was more likely delivering to a maid, perhaps, or a footman. Someone who was hired just for the night to tidy the house.

"This is quite the crush," Summer said, because it was expected. Then she added with a rush of genuine feeling, "The lemon tarts were absolutely divine."

Lady Bathurst beamed. "My husband said the heat would curdle them, but I kept them on ice until the very last moment.

He cried when he received the bill."

"I think it was worth it."

"There, you see? The Diamond approves. I shall tell him so."

Someone jostled her. "Oh, my apologies."

"Not to worry," Summer said. "It's rather a tight squeeze."

She worked her way to the back corner, claiming a tiny fraction of space and a mirror edged with pearls. She worked the nosegay into her palm as the chatter rose like the waves of the ocean all around her, hurried, hushed, frantic. Next to her foot was a large basket with clean, rolled handkerchiefs, just in front of a potted plant. This was similar to stealing for Aunt Georgie, if in reverse. The contrariness spoke to something inside of her.

If she dropped the nosegay in one of the baskets, there was a risk it would be carted off before it was claimed by the next Lark. If she tucked it inside one of the drawers, Lady Bathurst might go searching for something and find it first. There was a row of decorative glass vases on the mantelpiece, but reaching up to toss a nosegay into one would not be particularly subtle. On the other hand, there was a potted fern sitting under the window, right next to her. She flicked her wrist and let the nosegay fly into the little jungle of shadows created by the fronds.

Her heart pounded when she glanced around. No one noticed her. It was all lip salves and powder for sweat marks and whispering about who might be sitting where for supper.

"You do look smug," Lady Alice said to her as Summer rose to her feet. "Do you have a conquest in mind? Do tell."

Summer grinned—she couldn't help it. "Better."

"Better than Blackpool?" Alice returned with a snort. "Found yourself a fairy prince, have you? Because that's the only thing that would improve upon a man like Blackpool."

"Oh, we're not..." Except they were. But not like that.

And either way, she was suddenly not keen on the idea that he might choose someone else to spend his time with.

Alice pulled on her gloves. "If you like," she said, disbelief dripping from every syllable.

"I think you make a stunning pair," Miss Abbott said, starry-eyed. "Like two shiny thoroughbred horses."

Summer blinked. "Horses."

Miss Abbott looked suddenly appalled. "Not *horses*," she hastened to correct herself. "Roses?"

"Blackpool is a rose?" Summer couldn't wait to tell him.

"Stars? In the night sky? Shining!" She looked as though she might weep. "I'm not a very good poet."

Summer took pity on her. "Never mind, Miss Abbott. I take your compliment."

Offending Lady Summer was a very bad social faux pas. Summer would never retaliate over something so inconsequential, but there were too many hovering around them who would delight in it. "Miss Abbott," she added. "Would you sit with me at supper? I grow weary of the gentlemen, and I would like to hear more about your poetry."

Miss Abbott stuttered. "Thank you!"

Summer lowered her voice to a whisper. "Don't look so thrilled—they will eat you alive."

"Oh."

"Once you have your feet under you, show whatever feelings you like, but until then, you ought to be careful. These are not always gentle waters." She hated to tell anyone to temper themselves—she knew exactly how awful it felt to do. But she also knew how awful Society could be to young ladies, especially second daughters to minor barons.

"Thank you?" It came out as a question when Miss Abbott tried to temper her tone midway through.

"You might seek out Lady April. There is safety in numbers. Shall we?" Summer added as the ladies created a veritable river of bright silk and glittering jewels heading back to the event. They joined the flow, and Summer left the retiring room, the back of her neck prickling with the knowledge that she had just completed her first actual mission for the Crown as a lark and not as a temporary replacement because she happened to be on hand.

She mattered. What she did tonight, however small, *mattered*.

SUPPER PASSED WITHOUT incident, and then the dancing started up again, as well as games of cards. Blackpool had not yet arrived. She wondered what was keeping him, and if he'd managed to convince his idiotic superiors that they were wasting his talents. She might have to have a word with them herself.

She glanced out of the window for the third time, peering at the crowded street, the torchlights flickering along the path and gleaming at the windows of the other houses. There was so much movement, it was only a coincidence that had her spotting the figure under the lilac tree. She was well hidden, unlikely to draw attention.

But she was also familiar.

The Lark.

Summer could not help but think it did not bode well. Madeline was supposed to be in hiding across the water somewhere. Not on a busy street at the start of the Social Season where anyone might recognize her.

By the time Summer claimed her cloak and hurried outside, it had started to rain. Madeline, already bedraggled, now resembled a heroine from a gothic novel. Her auburn hair was in muddy tangles, and there was dirt under her fingernails and a rip in her dress. Summer pulled up her hood, making sure to pause by the tree. She flicked her cloak open as the wind picked up. Madeline did not need to be told. She ducked under the cloth and let Summer hurry her to the carriage. Everyone else outside was too busy running to avoid the rain, also crouching under cloaks and tree branches and makeshift umbrellas.

"Did you make your delivery?" Madeline asked when the carriage door shut behind them.

"Yes," Summer replied. "What happened to you?" She lifted her hand to her nose. "That is a pungent smell."

"No one cares to linger around someone with such an odor."

"I heartily agree."

"It makes me practically invisible. It's a trick you might need yourself if you continue to be a lark." Madeline's eyes were shrewd. "And you will, won't you?"

Summer wrinkled her nose, knowing she had no intention of stopping now. "Yes, but I hope to avoid whatever substance it is that you have encountered."

Madeline began to poke under the cushions. "You don't have any food around here, do you? I'm half starved."

"No, but we're nearly there."

They arrived at Rose House within minutes. Madeline's eyes widened, as did her smile. "No one would think to look for me in a pink house at the side of a duke's daughter." Her smile wavered. "I lived in a house like this once when I was very little."

"You lived in a house that looked like a macaron?"

"Not quite, but it was just as grand. Before my grandfather and my parents were taken to Madame Guillotine." She rubbed her hands, and dirt flaked off. "They wouldn't recognize me now."

Summer led her inside, making sure to dismiss the butler and the waiting footmen before they caught a whiff of her guest. Beatrix appeared in the hallway. Maggie was behind her, eating a tart. Before Summer could make any introductions, fictitious or otherwise, Beatrix coughed.

"You will tell us everything from a bath," she declared. "I cannot possibly think clearly when you smell like St. Giles gutter water."

Madeline sniffed, sighed. "Fair enough."

Chapter Twenty-One

B Y THE TIME the bathtub in Summer's room was filled, Madeline had eaten three asparagus tarts, an enormous wedge of cheese, and half a loaf of bread with apricot compote. Even Maggie looked impressed.

"What happened?" Summer asked as they waited on the other side of the screen. She'd removed her ruby necklace and her earrings, as they pinched. She'd also lit several of the beeswax candles and sprayed some of her perfume into the air. Madeline's disguise was a little too effective.

"I'm but a poor seamstress fallen on hard times."

Summer rolled her eyes. "Beatrix and Maggie know everything."

Beatrix smiled, just a little. "I should like that in writing."

Maggie snorted. She had changed out of her costume, but there were traces of rice powder along her hairline. "Why bother? You'll still remind us every single day."

"The rice powder didn't make you break out in a rash like your grease paint, now did it?" Beatrix pointed out.

"No."

"Well, there you go."

There was the sound of water from the bath, and scrubbing. Steam lifted, scented with rose soap. As if Aunt Georgie would have anything else in her pink house. "You were meant to keep your involvement a secret," Madeline said.

"Then your secret should not have put our friend in danger," Beatrix retorted, sounding harder than Summer had ever heard her.

"Truthfully, Beatrix and Maggie are both better equipped for this kind of work," Summer admitted, but it was hers now, and she was not going to give it up. Beatrix and Maggie turned toward her as one, glowering. She blinked. "What?"

"Stop it," Beatrix said.

"Never known a fancy lady not to demand compliments," Maggie muttered. "Do you think I'd trust just any toff while I'm dangling from the ceiling?"

"No?"

"Well then," Beatrix added. "That's enough of that."

Warmth she was not expecting spread through Summer's chest. "Oh."

"If you're all quite through," Madeline said drily, sloshing water onto the floor as she pulled herself out. "We have more pressing matters."

"Such as getting you out of London," Summer said. "Why aren't you already on some ship?"

"The docks were crawling with vermin," Madeline said, stepping out, wrapped in Summer's dressing gown. "I admit, I did not expect them to move so fast. Or have such numbers."

"I assume there's a reward," Beatrix supplied. "Most of them don't give a fig about the war."

"I thought the same," Madeline sighed. "But my contacts dried up, and those that stayed loyal would risk too much by helping me. There are eyes everywhere."

"Except here," Summer said.

"Here there are only pineapples," Madeline said. "And so much pink. Why is there so much pink?"

"Why not?" Summer shrugged. She crossed the room to the strawberry-painted desk, penning a very quick note. "I can get you out," she said.

"You can?"

"We'll get you to my brother's house in Cornwall. They can get you to the Guernsey or the Jersey Islands with a minimum of fuss." And by "they," she meant her smuggler sister-in-law.

"Where's that?" Maggie asked.

"It's a set of British islands in the Channel, very near France," Beatrix explained. "From there you could get to Belgium, the Netherlands. France, of course."

"France," Madeline said.

"Why?"

"My mother was French," she replied. "If I can get to France, I can be exactly who I am, Mademoiselle Pope, disgraced English spy. They will offer me money, and better yet, information. Eventually."

"And will you send that information to the English Crown?" Beatrix asked doubtfully. "Or stay where you are and betray those who betrayed you first?"

Madeline tilted her head. "Not a trace of judgment off you, is there, gel?"

Beatrix shrugged. "They came for you first."

"A nest of larks right under my nose and I never knew it," Madeline said regretfully. "What we could have accomplished..."

"We still can," Summer said.

"Perhaps," Madeline added. "*Peut-etre*. I suppose I ought to practice my French. But to answer your question..." She looked at Beatrix. "I have cousins on both sides of the war, murdering each other. The French government killed my family, but France is not only its government. It doesn't belong to Bonaparte either. He cares nothing for her."

"And you think England does?"

She snorted. "I am not a fool. I only want France to belong to France and England to belong to England. Preferably without rivers of the blood of my kin between them."

"Well, you'll never get anywhere with that red hair," Beatrix said. "Far too noticeable."

"Why do you think I rubbed dirt all over it?"

"Black walnuts would be much more efficient," Summer suggested. "It might run when you wash your hair and stain your neck, but not if you're very careful."

"We have some in the kitchen," Beatrix said.

Summer sent a message to her house, long neglected, asking the driver to bring the carriage and promising him a hefty tip for driving her guest to Cornwall immediately, without any questions. Beatrix returned with all of the necessary ingredients, and they made a paste for Madeline's hair. It turned her auburn hair to a dark, dull brown, changing her complexion completely.

"Do you have any widow's weeds?" Madeline asked. "A black veil over my face could only help."

Aunt Georgie was a bit thinner than Madeline, and a bit taller, but Summer decided they could make it work. "Give me a moment," she murmured before sneaking down the hall and into Aunt Georgie's dressing room. Lord Sutherland had made his wife promise she would wear black only for a month, instead of a year. He could not bear the thought of her having to wear dull colors—even the lavender of half mourning was an affront to him. For all his distractedness, he knew Aunt Georgie. Her love of bright colors and interesting art would be a better balm than societal conventions meant to advertise her grief. The vendetta was an added bonus.

Aunt Georgie's closet was a riot of colors and textures to rival anything Maggie wore in Astley's Amphitheatre. Or, indeed, anything worn at Drury Lane Theatre. There were traveling troupes with less flair. Pink dresses hung next to yellow pelisses trimmed in spangles, green ankle boots. Leaves were printed on muslin, with swans, cats. And in one case, tigers chased each other over a walking dress. And there, in the back, two dull black bombazine gowns, a day dress and a morning gown. The morning gown was embroidered with black pineapples. Summer reached for the day dress, a black veil, and a straw bonnet.

"A widow would never wear that bonnet," Aunt Georgie said

from the doorway, drinking red wine from a cup shaped like a duck at two in the morning. "If the friend you are smuggling out truly wants to fade into the background, try that dreadful bonnet with the bows. Lady Hayes sent it to me."

"How—"

"My dear, you are the not the first to help a woman escape in the dead of night—and, I daresay, you shan't be the last."

ELIOT RETURNED SHORTLY after they had spirited Madeline away in Summer's summoned carriage. He was quiet, making sure that the door made not a single sound when being shut. All of it ruined when he took a single breath. "What the hell is that smell?"

He heard a giggle from upstairs. It made him feel like he'd drunk two bottles of port. Only Summer could make him feel like that from an entire floor above his head. He loped up the stairs and found her dragging out a basket of wet linens, stinking of river mud and crushed walnuts from her chambers. Eliot paused. "Dare I even ask?"

Summer straightened. Her cheeks were pink from the exertion, her breasts straining at her neckline. He immediately wanted to drop to his knees and take them into his mouth.

"All in an evening's work for a lark," she said.

He noted the general state of disarray and the lingering, unfortunate odor and then tugged her backward into his chamber. It was a deep rose, offset with tiny golden flies painted on the wallpaper and scattered throughout. Summer made a face. "Aunt Georgie really went with an insect theme."

"Someone told her they were good luck," he explained fondly. "Remember? She went to that lecture on ancient Egyptian art. Golden flies were given as trophy rewards for military accomplishments."

"It's mildly horrifying."

"Worse than pink pineapples?"

"Don't be absurd. There is nothing *better* than pink pineapples." She smiled up at him expectantly. "How did it go? What happened? Did they agree that you would be a brilliant code breaker and apologize profusely?"

"Strangely enough, they did not," he said drily.

"Pity."

"I'll survive."

"Pity they are idiots, I mean."

He kissed her then, because how could he not? She was clever and beautiful and never believed the smiles the rest of the *ton* expected, never mind got flustered by them. She was warm in his arms, and her mouth tasted like peppermint tea. He licked at her until she moaned. He went hard immediately, with dizzying speed and intensity. When she rubbed against him, he swore he saw stars. The bed was close—a few steps and they could lose themselves.

She stepped back.

Away from the bed.

Away from him.

But she was smiling, even as she struggled to calm her breathing, which gave her away. "You owe me information, Lord Blackpool," she murmured, touching the tip of her tongue to her top lip.

Desire shot through him. She was teasing him. She knew exactly what it was doing to him.

Why did he like it so much?

She was blushing, just a little, and he was so fascinated by the sweet pink evidence that she was not unmoved that he let her push, let her play. Just for a little while. He wasn't made of stone.

Despite certain evidence to the contrary.

"Do I?" He advanced a step. Just enough to make her breath catch again. Her pupils expanded. It made him feel like a king. Like a supplicant. No one could do both to him with so little effort, and all at once.

"We had an accord."

"I don't recall agreeing to the terms."

"There were no terms," she said archly. "No quarter, remember?"

"Now, *that* I do remember. Just as I remember being very clear as to the consequences for teasing me."

"Prove it." She grinned, a flash of uncomplicated joy and a heavy dose of sass. It was the sass that made him want to grin back, but then the game was over and she had won. She loved to win. She loved even more to have to work hard for it. He knew that about her, had always known that. It was such a searing knowledge, one he could use to bring them both pleasure until they collapsed. Until she screamed his name.

And so he moved, advancing faster than before, faster than she anticipated. He had her pressed up against the garish wallpaper, and her mouth dropped open on a gasp. She squirmed against him, and it took every ounce of his willpower not to part her legs right then and there.

But that wasn't what she wanted.

He kissed her with long, deep strokes of his tongue until her head fell back. He dragged his mouth across her throat, scented with oranges and vanilla, over the pulse fluttering there and up to her ear, sucking just under the lobe. She shivered, gasping again. It was the sweetest music on earth, the sounds of her pleasure. Mozart, a king's orchestra, a choir of angels—none could compare.

"It's dangerous to tease me, plum," he growled in her ear.

She clutched at his arms, digging fingernails into his muscles as he continued to pin her with his body. "Promise?"

Fucking hell, she was perfect.

She'd already managed to undo the buttons of his breeches and dove her hand into his smalls, closing her fingers around his length. His spine went hot. She pulled him free, so that he bobbed heavily against his stomach, already hard for her.

And then she wriggled down, pushing him back so that she could sink her warm, wet mouth around him and suck. Hard.

Only once.

His hand hit the wall above her to steady himself.

She didn't suck again, only added a swirling, taunting lick around his head before standing up. Her eyes glittered and her lips were pink. "But first, you tell me everything."

He groaned, lust and amusement and something else entirely crashing through him. His chest was cracking open, like a mirror into shards that all reflected Summer. Only her.

"You are trying to kill me."

"Only if you ask nicely."

Chapter Twenty-Two

S HE HAD FOUND her new favorite thing.

Not winning at whist, or beating Eliot at billiards or parlor games—not even espionage.

It was this. Just this. Eliot hungry for her, eyes slightly feral, jaw twitching. The strength of him straining at the invisible ropes she created. Waiting.

He would pounce the moment she released him from the push and pull of this new contest between them.

She couldn't wait.

It would be even more delicious than this long, torturous pause that had her thighs going loose and liquid warmth gathering under her belly button. Lust threatened to consume her. She wanted to run her hands all over his body, the planes of his chest, the thick muscles of his thighs. Everywhere. Everything.

"Summer." He said her name harshly, and it was better than all of the sonnets ever composed for her.

She ducked under his arm and danced out of reach. "I want to know what the War Office said."

She could not have cared less. She would care very much tomorrow. Not tonight.

"I followed Glass a bit, but he did nothing out of the ordinary." He took a step in her direction, untying the knot in his cravat. "Before that, I was informed that I am not as far along as the War Office would like."

She was instantly incensed. "They are not doing any better. They haven't broken the cipher. And they abandoned Madeline."

"Did they? What exactly happened with your delivery?" he asked, the tendons of his neck prominent. He took off his coat, tossed it onto a chair. "When I looked in at the ball, you'd already left."

"It was perfectly uneventful," she assured him, taking a step back for every one that he angled toward her. "Until I found Madeline in the hedge."

He paused. "What?"

"She's fine. I brought her home."

"*What?*" Something darker, sharper honed to a point in his dark eyes.

"She needed an escape route. We dyed her hair and sent her to Cornwall."

He forced his shoulders to soften. "Of course you did."

"Someone had to."

"And that someone had to be you?"

He stalked her, graceful, beautiful. Deadly.

She loved every second of it. The hitch in her breath, the tingle in the back of her knees as something primal urged her to run. Just to see if he would chase.

He was already chasing her. Running her to ground.

She swallowed, sucked in her lower lip. He followed the movement, eyes flaring. "Careful, plum."

"Why?"

"You know why," he said. She did know why, and it made her thighs sing. "Are we done talking?"

"I suppose."

"*Plum.*" A thread of warning.

"Yes," she finally said, her voice softer than she'd thought it would be. How could she feel so powerful and yet so soft? Her neck prickled even as the rest of her threatened to melt. Eliot smiled. The smile that she was learning was just for her. The heat and pressure gathering low in her belly intensified. Her folds went soft and swollen and slick.

"I did warn you."

He didn't close the distance between them so much as he lunged for her. She'd barely turned on her heel and she was caught up in his arms. The room tilted, righted itself. A giggle threatened to burst from her. He caught it, growling. His tongue stroked hers, and he pulled at the sash that held her robe together. It fell open, revealing thin muslin. Her nipples were hard points against the fabric, and he brought his mouth to one, then the other. It was almost too much, not enough. Heat pulsed in her quim.

He lowered her to the bed. Not like a fine lady made of glass and gold, but like a feast he was starving, *desperate*, to devour. She pulled at his shirt until he removed it. His skin was so warm and soft over hard muscle. She barely had any time to touch him or stroke him. He placed a hand on her belly and held her down, looming over her, eyes lost in shadow. "My turn."

"But..." She reached for him, grazing his stomach. The muscles contracted under her fingertips.

"You had your fun," he said, using his knee to push her legs further apart. "You wanted to win, didn't you? Wanted to tease until I was mad with desire."

She squirmed. "Y-yes."

"Until you said the word. Isn't that right?"

"Yes."

"And what's the word, plum?"

He brushed against her folds, a taunt of a touch, a flick of her bud. She jolted, panting.

"What's the word, plum?"

"Eliot."

He raised an eyebrow, stern and strict. "Close."

She was pinned, on fire, desperate.

Loving it.

"Please," she finally begged. *"Please."*

He dragged her down the bed toward him in one powerful tug. He knelt, urging her legs over his shoulders. And then he feasted.

Soft licks, tiny bites, long, dragging draughts of her heat. Nibbling, sucking her bud into his mouth like a berry. Circling it with this tongue, circling, circling, circling. He used his fingers to draw her open, to fill her until she writhed and arched, reduced to nothing but heat and want and need. To nothing but his mouth and his hands coaxing her closer and closer to her climax.

And then he pulled away, wiping his chin with a grin better suited to a pirate. "I want to hear you scream my name."

She made a strangled sound, her fingers trailing down to her sex. The throb was too delicious, too tempting. Eliot grabbed her wrist, hard. "No. That's mine."

"Eliot." She squirmed.

"That orgasm belongs to me," he insisted. A long swipe of his tongue. "I decide."

And then he flipped her onto her stomach and drew her up, gripping her hips, his hardness at her bottom, slipping under to nudge her quim. "You say stop, we stop."

"I want more." She pushed back, trying to draw him in.

"You can have anything you want," he said before words became impossible.

He set a slow, deep pace, filling her, plunging, tilting her hips back so she took him even deeper. She could only dig her fists into the bedding, hold on as he took control. She could push back, but only a little. Mostly she moaned and gasped and held on.

When he bent forward to press a little closer against her, his hot, sweaty chest against her spine, his hand reaching for her bud, she could hold on no longer. She trembled through her orgasm, and Eliot's strokes stuttered, intensified, and then he was groaning, his nose buried in her neck.

There was only the dance of their bodies, the harsh song of their breaths, the wave of sensation traveling up her inner thighs and finally cresting in that exact place where they were one.

Chapter Twenty-Three

E LIOT COULD NOT sleep again, though he would happily sit by the fire and watch Summer snuggle into his bedsheets, warm and safe. She had not run away this time. He knew a flare of pride at that. And deep, deep satisfaction.

What was *not* satisfying, at present, was the incessant feeling that he was missing something obvious. It nibbled at him like a ferret. The list of names that had come into their possession, thanks to Summer's audacity, was too simple. No matter how he folded the parchment, it did not offer up any more clues, no sigil, no sketch of a London crossroads. Nothing. It was just a list of numbers.

And the cipher, the damned cipher—if it truly was just a book—also felt too straightforward. It had them stumped, so he supposed it had done the job. But espionage usually involved elaborate ciphers, invisible inks written in oak gall, riddles meant to be solved, if only by the right people.

Aidan was on the trail of two other members, but Glass remained their best lead, even thought he was too busy drinking port and losing his blunt to anyone willing to wager over a roll of the dice or a horse race to do much espionage. He was eagerly searching for a wealthy son-in-law and not much else. Eliot had followed him throughout London for days now, and it was always the same: club, gaming hell, gaming hell, club. Whist, vingt-et-un, dice. He'd once bet over whether or not a swan would bite at the Serpentine when offered grapes. And swans always bit.

Eliot smoothed the list, examining it once more. Always once more. Nothing notable about the ink, or the handwriting, or the paper. He made a sound of frustration in the back of his throat. Summer stirred in the big bed, under the gilt wallpaper. Not wanting to wake her, Eliot padded on bare feet out to the hall and down to the library.

His work waited under the corner window. The chair was, naturally, bonbon pink. On the table, a small stack of the books he had taken from Glass: two volumes of poetry, a manual on horse breeding. Thoroughly unhelpful, no matter how many times he used them. April had the copy of *Debrett's Peerage*. Eliot had not had to nick it—Aunt Georgie had her own copy right there under the window. *Debrett's Peerage* was too obvious, anyway. It was pages and pages of names of the British aristocracy. Hardly subtle.

And yet just simple enough to stump them.

The gilded letters caught his eye. Why hadn't he noticed how many copies there were? The one he used was kept in the drawing room for easy perusal. But there were eight more copies here in the library, bound in pink leather to match the house, slightly dusty, suggesting they had not been opened in some time.

Cursing, he pushed out of his chair.

Debrett's Peerage was published in two volumes. That much he knew. But it was also published every couple of years, sometimes annually. And Glass did not seem the type to rush out and purchase a new copy. Especially now.

Aunt Georgie, however, had all of them.

The first volume of the previous version offered only gibberish when used as a cipher.

The second volume, however, after painstaking translation, was far more fruitful.

Miss Esther Smith.

Lady Elizabeth Warwick.
Miss Cecily Yardley.
He'd done it.
He'd broken the cipher.

SUMMER WOKE IN the middle of the night, alone in the wide bed, as the fire burned cheerfully. Wherever Eliot had gone off to, he had thought to stoke the flames for her before leaving in case the morning proved damp. And as his breeches were still in a pile on the floor, he had not gone far.

She rolled over, enjoying the twinges in well-used muscles. She enjoyed it even more when Eliot slipped back into the room in his dressing gown, idly tied, chest muscles on display.

"Go back to sleep," he murmured when she stirred.

His eyes blazed. He looked different. She sat up. "No chance of that."

"Instincts of a lark." He laughed softly.

"What's happened?" She wrapped the sheet around her and stood up. "Did you find proof?"

He shook his head but did not look one bit defeated. "Better."

"Better?"

"I broke the cipher."

"You did?" The surge of pride she felt on his behalf startled her. "Of course you did," she added. "I knew you would."

"You're the only one." He pulled on his clothes, breeches, lawn shirt, and a coat. No waistcoat or cravat, no summoned valet. Not her Eliot. Society's Lord Blackpool, perhaps, but not her Eliot. He kissed her quickly, as if he could not help himself. "I have to go and warn them. Can't wait until morning."

"Of course not," she said. She desperately wanted to go with him, but there was no time. "Go."

But as soon as Eliot left the house, Summer contorted herself into a twist to secure her stays, pulled a walking dress over her head, and then sent a footman to hire her a hackney. She chose Tom, whom, she knew perfectly well, Eliot had sent to shadow her. He sat next to the driver, refusing to leave her to her own devices.

She went straight to Lord Glass's townhouse because she was not an idiot—and also because she was not an idiot, she waited patiently inside the carriage. She would do very little good by either barging into the house or sneaking into it so late at night alone. She had asked the driver to wait just down past the Glass house, where an event was clogging traffic with carriages. They were just far enough not to be trapped and also not to be noticed.

It did not take long for Eliot to arrive, having dispatched his warnings to the compromised larks. A knock sounded sharply on her carriage door. "Summer, open the door," he said.

She pushed the curtain aside and smiled at him through the window. "Blackpool."

He shook his head. "Just come on."

She practically flew out onto the sidewalk. "You're not going to leave me behind?"

"Would it do any good?"

"Of course not."

"Well, there you have it, then." He glanced at her out of the corner of his eye. "And I wouldn't do that to you."

She reached out and squeezed his hand. He really was better at compliments than anyone in London. England. Europe, even. "Thank you." She shot Tom a grin where he waited on the box. "See, Tom? I told it would be fine."

Tom did not reply.

"I think he's afraid of you," Summer murmured.

"He's afraid of *you*," Eliot corrected her before adding, "Glass was detained at his club. I made sure of it. It ought to buy us just enough time to have a proper search of his house. Finally find some solid evidence before we accuse him."

"What about the servants? And April, if she's at home?"

"Most of them will be asleep at this hour. Two spies like us should be able to avoid the few who aren't, wouldn't you say?"

He had called her a spy. Properly.

It was better than a proposal.

Not that she expected him to propose. Or that she had an eye to marriage. She would never marry Lord Blackpool.

She might well marry Eliot, though.

Now there was a surprising thought.

Focus, Summer.

She *was* focused, thank you very much.

Not on that.

Fine.

"What are you muttering to yourself?" Eliot asked, amusement plain on his handsome face. Very handsome face. *Too* handsome face.

"I'm not muttering," she *absolutely* muttered.

The house loomed quiet and dark before them, with a single light shining through the window above the front door and another in the family wing. Clouds hung low, softening the edges. Mist curled up from the damp ground to meet them, providing adequate cover.

Eliot went down the lane to the mews, staying close to the gardens along the house. Large hydrangea bushes and lilac trees marched in a row. Summer ducked under the leaves, keeping her steps light. The mews were quiet; Lord Glass had taken the carriage and the driver with him to his club. "Beatrix says there's always someone in the kitchens," Summer whispered when Eliot appeared to be heading for the back door. "At any time of the night in any household."

"In that case..." He paused, looked at the many windows lined up behind the bushes. "How do you feel about proper housebreaking?"

"Extremely good about it, actually."

"You do not disappoint."

Neither did he. She did not see how he did it, but with some kind of tool he removed from his coat pocket, he lifted the window latch within seconds. "You are definitely teaching me how to do that," she said.

"Marry me and I will."

He didn't wait for her response. It was a good thing, as her mouth gaped open in a most unladylike way and she actually had to shake her head to get her wits back in order. He must be joking. Or drunk.

He was probably drunk.

He didn't smell like spirits. Only like cedar and rain. Like Eliot.

Sleep deprived, then.

He poked his head into the dark room, looked from right to left, and then reemerged, clearly satisfied. "Shall we?"

She blinked. A lot. Too much. "Get married?"

He smirked. "Break into the house."

"Oh. Right."

He scooped her up into his arms. His nose brushed her cheek. "But my offer stands, plum."

Because she tingled from the roots of her hair to the tip of her toes, she sniffed. "That was hardly an offer."

"You said no flattery."

She was both very comfortable against his chest and very uncomfortable. She wanted to squirm, wanted to wriggle until she was facing him, legs on either side of his hips. *Pressing* into him. He growled, just a little, into her ear, as if he knew exactly what she was thinking. His arms tightened around her. "Still teasing, plum?" His breath was warm against her throat.

She lightly scraped her nails through the hair at the nape of his neck. "I'm sure I don't know what you mean."

"You absolute menace," he breathed.

"Why, thank you."

He turned and angled her feet into the open window, supporting her as she slid through. It would have been a very ungraceful affair without him. She'd have landed on her face.

She made a mental note to practice sneaking through windows. She'd ask Maggie, who could contort herself like a knot of braided bread.

Eliot dropped her into Glass's study. He followed suit, making it look easy. As if he'd done it a hundred times. Mayfair really had no idea how it underestimated him. She had done so as well.

The study was even sparser than it was the night of the ball. The ledgers open on Glass's desk suggested he had not suddenly become more adept at either racing horses or betting on them. Nor card games. They found nothing else and stepped into the dark hallway. When no one came running at them screaming, "Thief," Summer allowed herself to breathe. It turned into a strangled "gah" when she came eyeball to eyeball with *The Red Mare*.

Something about that painting still bothered her.

And it wasn't just the truly wretched and slightly lopsided horse, who looked resigned to her fate. It was unlike the others in a way that made no sense. Lord Glass did not have a whimsical bone in his body. And he had sold everything he could get his hands on. Clearly the poor red mare had no value beyond the possibly sentimental, and Glass was also not the sentimental sort. He preferred classical art, pieces with cachet. Something to brag about. Something to sell. Perhaps April had painted it? Summer looked closer but could see no signature beyond a faded scrawl that might have been a name or a distressed ladybug. Hard to say.

Eliot motioned to her with a jerk of his head. She fell into step behind him. The footman set to wait at the front door for Glass was asleep in his chair, head lolling on his shoulder. Summer passed him, her spine prickling the entire way up the staircase. More paintings were missing from the walls. The candles in the sconces had burned down to nubs, and they were not the expensive beeswax Glass had reserved for the ballroom. Everything about it screamed that something dodgy was afoot.

Besides her and Eliot, of course.

The upper floor was deserted, with a lamp burning on a table cleared of all decorative art. Eliot headed to a door on the left. "His valet might be waiting for him in the dressing room," he warned under his breath. "Likely asleep, but step carefully."

She nodded to let him know she understood. Her lady's maid Elsie slept like the dead on the nights she waited for Summer to return from some entertainment or another. Hopefully Glass's valet was the same.

The bedchamber was large and well appointed, hung with velvet at the windows and over the bed. It was muted and elegant and exactly as expected. Not a hint of a fish-man or a red mare. The floor was faded around a square where a carpet had recently been removed. Nothing else looked as though it had been taken away. Glass clearly reserved any luxury left for himself. Again, not surprising. Mayfair was Mayfair.

Eliot crept to the bed and searched under the mattress. He shook her head at her questioning glance. If she were an entitled, boring rat who stole art from elderly widows, where would she hide information on a treacherous auction? She checked the mantelpiece and around the grate for any sections that looked different. Nothing moved; no secret compartments were revealed. She kept searching, and the pounding of her heart slowed in her ears as she grew more accustomed to their subterfuge.

Nothing under the seat cushions, nothing inside his collection of snuffboxes, nothing tucked above the windows or the door.

Nothing.

Eliot shook his head again, frustrated. He nodded to the door. They were risking discovery with every minute they lingered.

Still, once back downstairs, outside the study, she paused.

"What is it?" Eliot asked, glancing at the now-snoring footman.

"It's this painting."

"Now is not the time to steal it, however much you want to give it to Aunt Georgie."

She rolled her eyes, though the thought had occurred to her. "Not that."

"What, then? We can't linger."

"I know." She ran her fingers over the painting, trying to

figure out why she was so convinced there was something to find. The paint was no thicker or thinner than it should be, the canvas no smoother or bumpier. Eliot watched her for a beat before lifting the frame off the wall so she could properly inspect it. She didn't have to.

A folded piece of parchment floated to the parquet floor.

"I'll be damned," he said, peering at the backing of the painting before putting it back on its hook. Summer scooped up the parchment, and they ducked into the study. The light was poor but not impossible to read by. She unfolded it, pulse hammering in her ears again. This was it. She had found something.

To trade the Lark for a wren,
Be fleet of foot to where the Charlies wait.
Don't be early, don't be late,
Or I'll send these birds to Amiens.

"He is clearly not a poet." Summer wrinkled her nose. "At least it's short. And not a sonnet."

"Temple Bar," Eliot said, his code-breaking mind already leagues ahead. "It was designed by Christopher Wren. Lark for a Wren." And it had statues of King Charles the First and the Second.

Later, when it was appropriate, she would remind herself how extraordinarily attractive he was when his eyes sharpened that way, finding threads other missed. Seeing things others did not even think to look for. As he'd done with her, time and time again. Only it had taken her some time to realize it.

"When?"

"The Treaty of Amiens was broken on May eighteenth, last year."

"I see." She did not.

"Today is also the eighteenth. The auction is tonight."

Chapter Twenty-Four

S UMMER WOULD HAVE preferred to be dressed for taking down the auction of a traitor selling and buying war secrets.

Instead, she was dressing for a masquerade gala in order to steal the last of the art back for Aunt Georgie.

As far as compensations went, it was not bad.

Aunt Georgie had insisted the safety and security of England was not more important than the safety and security of her art. Or her girls, as she had taken to calling Summer, Beatrix, and Maggie.

Taking down a gentleman in the heart of Mayfair was vastly different than taking down a room full of traitors. Not that Aunt Georgie would ever imply that they could not do it. In fact, she had already suggested that if Eliot was not done by the time they had reclaimed her things, they ought to go help him. He had turned white, then green. The image of Aunt Georgie storming such a meeting was entirely plausible and would no doubt end badly.

Lord Glass was apprehended by the War Office and secured for questioning. The rumor about town was that he had fled for the country after losing six thousand pounds to Lord Blackpool. Eliot had spread the rumor. Summer had helped. A visit to the mantua maker, a whisper here, a whisper there, a turn about Hyde Park, and the *ton*'s most notorious gossips were informed.

All of Mayfair followed within the hour.

Being *Lady Summer* was rather useful.

"I'm sorry to miss it," Eliot said from her doorway.

Summer met his eyes in the looking glass in front of her. Her maid secured the last of her hairpins. "Thank you, Elsie."

Their gazes did not break, not when Elsie curtsied, biting back a smirk, nor when she slipped out of the room. Eliot tugged the door closed behind him, still watching Summer. She finally turned and rose to her feet. She wore a white ball gown, exceedingly simple in its design. The overdress would come next, and her mask.

"Beautiful."

"I am nowhere near ready."

"And yet you look like a queen," he said softly. He flashed a lopsided grin. "A fierce queen ready to run people through with her sword," he amended. "Not at all beautiful, actually. Practically plain. I don't know what I was thinking."

She sniffed with mock primness. "Thank you."

"When are you going to let me tell you that you are stunning?" he asked roughly. "That you take my breath away every single day."

She was the one fighting for her breath. "You're very good at that. I suppose you ought to be by now."

"You're implying I've been practicing?"

"Haven't you been?" Through swaths of ladies since he was a lad.

"Does that bother you?" A line furrowed between his brows.

"Actually, it doesn't." It was part of who he was. He meant every compliment he tossed out, easy as birdseed. Even when he had driven her mad with his teasing and his dares, she had trusted him. He didn't cheat. Not with games, or puzzles, and definitely not with his word.

"Shall I finally tell you why I call you plum?" he asked. "Instead of darling or dove. Other than the fact that you would roll your eyeballs clear out of your head if I called you dove?"

She fought a smile. "Go on."

"Because of that day we made a wager to see who could climb the highest in that plum tree—do you remember?"

It was after her second Season. She'd had another fight with her mother and was feeling both frustrated and maudlin, wandering the orchard in a gray mood. Eliot had insisted she could never reach the top of the tree before he could.

He always seemed to find her when she needed him to.

"You did it on purpose," she realized.

"You looked as though you were about to cry," he said. "And you never cry. Not even that time you sprained your ankle when we had that footrace into the sea. Besides, they were the last plums on the tree, and I knew you were lighter than me and had a better chance of reaching them."

"I had no idea you were so sneaky, even then."

"It was worth it. We picked all of the plums, and we sat in the grass and ate them all. They were warm from the sun. You even smiled at me." He was standing right in front of her now. "The juice ran down your wrist, and you licked it off." He pressed his fingers to the pulse on the inside of her wrist. "I'd never wanted anyone more than I wanted you in that moment," he said. "And every time I've eaten a plum in all of the years since, I've known it wouldn't be as sweet as you would be in my mouth."

She swallowed again. Hard.

He brushed his mouth over hers, licked at her lower lip.

"I've been starving ever since."

Heat burst in fiery sparks in her belly. She had no idea he could say such things, or that such things would make her gasp with want. Her nipples pebbled; her quim swelled and slicked.

"You'll always be the girl who climbed the highest tree," he added. "Give them hell."

She tilted her head back to meet eyes of the richest, darkest brown. She wanted to sink into his gaze. Drown in it. "And you'll always be the boy who knew exactly why I needed to climb it."

He kissed her hard, quick. Possessive.

And then he grinned. "Whoever gets back here last has to marry the other."

She stared at him as he stepped into the hall. "You can't just *dare* me to marry you."

"Can't I?"

His laugh floated up the stairs behind him.

Chapter Twenty-Five

THE MAYFAIR ART Collectors Society, despite being plagued by break-ins and thieves, had pulled off the affair of the Season, as promised. Mayfair descended in droves, like honeybees to the last garden. They came to see the art and to be seen in return. The invitations were clear: *dazzle us.*

There was a woman in a white dress that turned into a swan. Another wore a shawl of gold feathers. Her companion had pinned silk butterflies from the top of her hair to the toes of her shoes. Another lady resembled nothing so much as Lady Macbeth, in a faintly medieval dress with her long evening gloves covered in tiny red glass beads that shimmered a little too much like blood. "Bravo," Summer murmured. Lady Macbeth grinned and offered a small bow.

Aunt Georgie, naturally, wore a green dress and a towering wigged painted to look like a pineapple. A vengeful pineapple who had already threatened two members and "accidentally" drilled her cane in the foot of another. The man would be limping for days. Possibly weeks.

Aunt Georgie preened.

Beatrix had opted to disguise herself as any other aristocratic woman, which would afford her better access tonight than acting the housekeeper. Between Summer's closet, Beatrix's own skills, and Maggie's costuming experience, she was stunning, even if she clearly hated it.

"You look perfect," Summer had told her when she found Beatrix in the front hall, uncharacteristically wringing her hands.

"I look like a *lady*." She grimaced as if she'd bitten into something truly revolting. She paused. "Sorry."

Summer shrugged, unoffended. "You *do* look like a lady." And she was beginning to realize all of the ways in which that could be valuable. She'd felt constricted by other people's assumptions and expectations for too long. She'd been raised to be a lady. It was her job.

But tools could be more than one thing. A hammer could drive a nail through a wall and pluck one free as well. She couldn't stop being a duke's twin sister. But she could finally, finally wield the position instead of having it wielded unto her. She did not wish to be ungrateful. There were women sewing by lamplight in the street not ten minutes from here with their bellies cramping with hunger and their fingers stiff with work. But nor did she wish to be Society's doll.

She was right back where she started: in the Mayfair Art Collectors Society's gallery townhouse, ready to steal art for Aunt Georgie.

And yet so much had changed.

She had changed.

And her relationship with Eliot. She'd always thought he did not take her seriously, when it turned out he was the only one who did.

Enough to dare her to marry him.

As if she needed the wager.

"Don't stand so close to the chandelier," Beatrix said. "You'll burn my eyeballs clear out of their sockets."

With Elsie's painstaking help, Summer glittered.

Literally.

She had topped her white gown with a long pelisse, also in white. From neckline to hem, cuff to cuff, crystals gleamed and shone. It was like wearing ice. Or fairy dust. Diamonds marched around her throat, more crystal beads on her gloves. She had added a half-mask, also beaded.

Lord Dalton bowed to her. "Ah, Lady Summer. A diamond of the first water, as always."

Summer curtsied, her customary red lips curving in a smile. "You are too kind."

Let them see what they expected to see and they would look no further.

"So that's why you're so shiny," Beatrix muttered before losing herself in the crowd. Maggie was already on the rooftop, watching the London smog eat at the stars until it was time for her to swing into action.

Summer wondered what Eliot was doing right now. Was he safe? Had he found the auction?

She allowed Lord Dalton to escort her into the ballroom, showing her all of the new pieces up for display. She paused in front of a small velvet box where tiny portraits no bigger than a peach were pinned. The one on the left belonged to Aunt Georgie. It was too ridiculous looking not to. A little girl with a pet dog who looked like nothing so much as a demon crossed with a duck.

She waited until Beatrix found her again, passing behind her, just a little bit too closely. Summer stumbled a bit theatrically, gasping loudly. Lord Dalton caught her elbow. People turned to stare. Summer fanned herself with a charming smile. "Goodness, how exciting."

Behind her, she nicked the portrait off the pedestal and dropped it into Beatrix's waiting hand, angled behind her back. Summer immediately moved away, chattering and keeping the attention on her. Beatrix tucked it in her hair and stopped to admire a perfectly presentable landscape of a garden.

One down, three to go.

She spotted Aunt Georgie's salt cellar easily, mostly because Aunt Georgie herself stood in front of it, her chin lifted stubbornly, her eyes suspiciously shiny. The salt cellar was gilt copper and shaped like the head of a roaring lion. Its eyes were uncanny.

Summer reached her just as Lord Tottenham did, Lady April at his side. "Lady Sutherland," he boomed. "You look positively scrumptious."

She blinked once, swallowed, before replying, "Oh, you."

"I insist you dance with me," he continued. "You are the only interesting thing here. All these faded landscapes." He shuddered theatrically. "Positively dreary."

Aunt Georgie's smile widened, deepened. "Of course, Lord Tottenham."

Summer stopped herself from kissing him right there in the middle of the stuffy ballroom under three paintings of family cows and a sketch by Leonardo da Vinci.

Lady April looked overwhelmed but determined. She curt-sied. "You are the perfect mouse!" Aunt Georgie exclaimed, and she was not being facetious.

April wore a debutante's white gown, but her ribbon sash was the gray of mouse fur. Her jewelry dripped with pale pink stones that matched the pink satin of the mouse ears she had tucked into her hair. Her fan was painted with little mice pouncing on triangles of cheese. "Someone once told me that I should be myself," April murmured, glancing at Summer. "And use it to my advantage."

"Little mouse," Summer approved. "They will never see you coming."

"Next time I shall dress as Joan of Arc."

"I cannot wait to see it."

Lord Tottenham winked at her. "Are you going to honor me with a dance as well, Lady Summer? An old man like me."

"Gladly," she twinkled. She lifted the dance card attached to her wrist and took out the little pencil from her reticule. "You may have your choice, sir."

He twinkled back at her guffawing. "Let's kick young Ash out of the third spot. He'll only step on your toes."

"My toes and I thank you."

The tiny pencil was dwarfed in his large hand as he made a big show of writing his name on her card. All of the dance cards were decorated with a watercolor silhouette of a Roman-style garden folly at sunset. Dignified, pretty.

Summer desperately wanted to paint pineapples on every single one she saw. Pink cheetahs. A duck-demon.

The music swelled, and the space cleared in the center of the room so that couples could dance under hundreds of years of art. Lord Tottenham led his granddaughter into the first dance, shouting compliments as they went. Summer added false names to the empty spots remaining on the card. She was here for proper criminal activity, after all.

Something about Lord Tottenham's name made her take a second look. She recognized his handwriting. It was familiar, but in a way that did not make sense. They had never danced before, nor had they cause to exchange letters. But she knew the swoop of the *h*, the oversized *o*. She had seen it before.

On the list of spies.

Those names and the cipher of numbers had been inked in his hand.

The Temple Bar riddle.

She was sure of it.

Lord Glass wasn't the traitor. His father-in-law was.

And that meant the auction wasn't at Temple Bar, but with Tottenham here at the masquerade, at an event where everyone's faces would be disguised, and no one would think twice about it. Brilliant.

Except Eliot was not here. He was on a wild goose chase. Tottenham had cleared the field for himself.

And she did not know who else to trust.

But she did know one thing, through to her bones in that very moment with shining clarity.

Diamonds did *more* than shine.

They cut.

Through everything.

Something was wrong.

It wasn't just that every part of Eliot wanted to be at Summer's side as she ventured into the gala. He wanted to see her at her work, wanted to be there when she hid a triumphant grin. Wanted to make damn sure no one trifled with her.

That was a given.

That the auction was taking place at Temple Bar was something else.

None of this sat right.

The decorated gate arched over the street where it changed from the Strand to Fleet Street, dividing Westminster from the City of London. Three arches, niches for statues of King James and King Charles II, ornamental stonework, and, thankfully, no severed heads on pikes. Not anymore. It was both out of the way and very much *in* the way. The fog, the leftover rain shining over the mud, the smell of horses. He catalogued it all, and it still felt off.

He ducked under the archways, where it smelled strongly of the Thames and piss. Something scurried away in the shadows, a mouse or a rat.

The way the night was going, he'd bet on a rat.

He climbed up to the top, already expecting it to be empty. It was. Nothing but shadows and puddles of water.

Lord Glass's involvement had always felt too obvious. If he was clever enough to track down the Lark and three other spies, why was he not clever enough to use someone's else art to deliver messages? Why keep clues to the auction in his house, relatively easy to find? And why choose Temple Bar, of all places, he wondered as he dropped back down to the ground.

He was being played.

He didn't have evidence. Not yet. Only the lifting of the hair at the back of his neck.

And the scrape of a shoe on the sidewalk.

He bent his knees, dropping a knife into his palm. A hackney rolled by, oblivious. Someone shouted with laughter from a pub across the way. The sound stretched, distorted between the stones and the wet mud and the thick glass windows.

Eliot whirled just in time to stop the descent of a cudgel on the back of his head.

The block of the blow stuttered through his forearm. His assailant was large, face hidden under the brim of an old hat. He didn't waste time cursing, only attacked again.

If Eliot was in the crosshairs, did that mean Summer was as well? Even now, moving through a masquerade gala with every titled family in London? He hadn't put enough guards on her. An army would not be enough.

Rage and fear for her safety boiled his blood.

He ducked the next attack and came up behind the man, viciously kicking the back of his kneecap. A window was shut and locked somewhere above them. No one was likely to interfere.

Good.

"Who sent you?" Eliot snapped, punching him in the throat. He gagged, slashing back with his own dagger. The tip sliced through Eliot's sleeve, grazing his arm. Enough to sting, not enough to incapacitate. The hit to his jaw was a great deal more incapacitating. His head snapped back. *Head in the game, Blackpool.*

The man wasn't going to answer him anyway. Eliot danced back. "How much is he paying you?"

"Quit your yammering."

"I'll pay you twice as much."

A snort of disbelief. But the barest of pauses, too. Interest. He could work with that.

They circled each other, blood dripping at their feet.

"I want that name." Whoever had sent him here to this bloody trap wasn't buying a cipher. He was selling it. Elsewhere. And Eliot was running out of time.

"How much do you want it, bruv?"

Eliot named an astronomical fee.

The man's eyes widened. "You're lying."

Eliot tossed a handful of coins from his pocket at him. "Consider this my deposit."

The man caught them, whistling at the weight.

"Now talk."

"Didn't tell me his name, but he was a fancy toff, like you. Big old man, with a white beard. Size of a bloody house."

Eliot knew only one man who fit that description.

And it wasn't Lord Glass.

His informant was too busy staring down at the coins in his palm to see him coming. Eliot clubbed him in the temple with the hilt of his dagger. He dropped like a stone. "Don't worry," Eliot muttered. "You'll get your money." He didn't have time to fuss over details, to convince the man to come with him, to do anything but get to the bloody gala, where Summer might right now be dancing with a murderer.

He hailed a hackney and pushed the unconscious man inside. "Too much wine," he called up to the driver, in case an explanation was needed. It wasn't. The driver did not care in the slightest. He accepted directions to the gala and then closer to Soho. Let Aidan deal with him. He'd arrived trussed up like a goose for the Christmas table.

Eliot's duty would be done, and it was nothing to what he would do for Summer.

Anything.

Everything.

Chapter Twenty-Six

SUMMER FOLLOWED TOTTENHAM, blood rushing in her ears. There was no time to send word to Eliot. Or the War Office, if she even had the first idea how to do such a thing. Or a magistrate.

She would have to settle for the footman following her around, eyes nearly as sharp as the dagger she was certain was on his person somewhere. In the last week, Summer had tasked Elsie with sewing pockets for all of her dresses, even the evening gowns. She carried her own knife, a bundle of long needles, and a wedge of wood carved with a lark, inspired by Madeline. None of which solved her immediate problem.

She kept her smile fixed as guests greeted her on her dash out of the ballroom. Beatrix appeared at her side. "What is it?"

"You are positively supernatural, and I love you for it. Come with me."

The footman followed, carrying his silver tray clinking with champagne glasses. He wasn't fooling anyone. Summer knew perfectly well he was here at Eliot's behest. "Keep up, Tom."

Tottenham had gone upstairs. At least he was still in the building. And he was not rushing, moving only with the measured pace of an old earl. And a traitor.

Summer scooped a mask from the basket provided by the society for guests and turned to the footman. "Tom, find

Blackpool."

"Your ladyship?"

"There's no *time*." She lowered her voice. "I know he set you to watch me. We need him here, *now*." Whomever he was chasing, Glass or some other decoy sent by Tottenham, he wasn't safe. "He *needs* you. Temple Bar. Tell him it's Tottenham."

When he turned on his heel, she dashed up the stairs, Beatrix in tow. "Tottenham," she murmured. "He's good. He was not even on my list. That is vexing, I don't mind telling you."

"He wasn't on anyone's list. But he's here now, instead of holding an auction at Temple Bar."

"Misdirection."

"Exactly."

"And here we are in a house full of people in disguise. Brilliant, really."

"We need to be *more* brilliant."

She scoffed. "Naturally." She peered down the empty hallway. "That way." She pointed right. "The flames in the sconces are still flickering."

Summer paused. She had dressed to be noticed. She glittered like the Thames after an ice storm. "We need to know who is at that auction." The list had been decoded, thanks to Eliot. It should be useless now, thank God.

"I'll go in," Beatrix offered.

Summer shook her head. "It has to be me. They'll all be in costume, but I'm likely to know at least some of them well enough to be able to tell. Hopefully. If nothing else, I can sketch their likenesses afterward." She stepped into the nearest parlor and turned her back. "Unhook me."

In a matter of minutes, Summer stood in a white ball gown like any other. The spangled overdress hung on the back of a chair. Her jewelry was tucked into one of her pockets, her mask hidden, discarded on the mantel. In its place she set the mask she had taken from the basket. It covered most of her face. No one would ever assume someone so simply dressed was the glittering

Lady Summer.

She handed Beatrix the chunk of wood from her pocket. "Jam this under the door and lock us in. Just in case."

"I'm not locking you inside with those people."

"You have to. We can't let them get away."

"Blackpool is going to murder me," Beatrix muttered.

THERE WERE SEVERAL parlors and bedrooms to choose from down the right end of the hall. Summer forced herself to walk easily, as if she knew where she was going and was perfectly in the right. That, at least, she had years of training in. Hard to believe she found something to be grateful for in her mother's exacting requirements. But when she floated into the only room with a partially closed door, no one questioned her.

They turned to stare, but that, too, she was accustomed to.

Apparently, being a lady had much in common with being a spy.

The morning room was sparsely furnished, mostly with chairs and crates of paintings along the back wall. There were four gentlemen and two ladies seated. No one spoke. Summer took her own seat and distracted herself from the swirl of nerves in her belly by seeking out little details. The gentleman in the front row by the window tapped his foot nervously. The woman next to him wore a bonnet with a veil over her face. Summer wished it were Madeline, come back to help her, but knew she was on her own.

The man directly in front of her was dressed like most of the guests—black breeches, black coat, white gloves. She could not see the color of his hair under his hat. He smelled like cloves.

Lord Hayes.

He chewed cloves on a daily basis for his aching teeth.

The last man she did not recognize, but the other woman had to be Lady Cole. There was nothing obvious about her dress, or what little was visible of her arms and decolletage, except for a tiny, faded scar on her collarbone where she'd been bitten by the family cat.

Summer's heartbeat calmed. She could do this. She was a lark now. And she had Beatrix lurking nearby.

When Tottenham entered, he too wore a mask. He had disappeared long enough to shave off his iconic whiskers. His collar was damp, his chin ruddy. She would not have known it was him, despite his size. He was synonymous with those white whiskers. He was clever. It did not bode particularly well. Nor did the very large man who followed him inside and then closed the door, standing in front of it with crossed arms. He was equipped with various weapons, of course. Summer was down to what amounted to a pocketful of sharp sticks.

It would have to do.

"Let's get started." Tottenham modulated his voice, softening it. "Highest bidder. Start at eight thousand pounds."

Lord Hayes raised his hand. "Eight thousand, two hundred."

The veiled woman raised hers. "Eight thousand, three hundred."

The price climbed to an astronomical fifteen thousand pounds within minutes. Summer tried to think of what to do when they all realized they were locked inside. What if the footman hadn't found Eliot? Worse, what if he was wounded?

She'd wound Tottenham right back.

Severely.

"The cipher to the gentlemen in the back row for seventeen thousand pounds," Tottenham said. "The rest of you may go. Pleasure doing business with you."

Lord Hayes stood up. "What if we don't want to go?"

"I'll make you," the guard at the door said. Flatly. As if he was bored. It was faintly chilling. Even without the fact that he could probably crush any of their skulls like a melon. He reached for the doorknob. "Now get out."

The door did not open.

He pushed harder.

Summer edged backward, away from the cluster of disgruntled spies and conspirators.

"Door's stuck," the guard rumbled.

"Break it down," Tottenham ordered him.

The door did not break. The top rattled but held. The trapped conspirators began to mutter and curse. The air changed.

This had seemed like a good idea at the time.

It did not take long for someone to throw the first punch. It was the veiled lady, and she had a decent right hook. It was not enough to take out the guard. It only served to annoy him. One of the other men leapt into the fray. Daggers made appearance from pockets, reticules, a boot.

Behind them, the window slid open. No one noticed the woman hanging upside down through the dark glass. Not even Summer, who might have expected it. She was too busy backing away, keeping her chair in front of her like a lion tamer. Or an Astley's Amphitheatre performer, as it were.

Lord Hayes and a second gentleman lay sprawled in a bloody heap. Lady Cole had stabbed the guard in the thigh with a very long, very vicious hatpin. Summer took note of that trick. For later.

Assuming there would be a later.

At the moment she was more concerned with the very sharp blade at her throat.

She had backed right into Tottenham. Or he had maneuvered toward her. She supposed it hardly mattered with a knife at her throat. Still, her pride hoped for the former.

Why did she feel so calm? So hot and cold at the same time? Fear sizzled under her skin, prickling the hairs on her arms. "Don't," she said.

Tottenham froze. "Lady Summer."

Bollocks.

You'd think taking down a traitor would grant you a little luck from the Fates. Just a little.

Enter Eliot Howard, Earl of Blackpool.

Through the window.

HE HAD HOPED his entrance might be slightly more on the stealthy side instead of dramatic, but once an earl, always an earl.

It did not help that when he saw Summer, a roar built in his chest fit to demolish the entire building. The entire block. "Get the hell away from her, Tottenham."

Tottenham jerked at the sound of his name, but he didn't release her.

Eliot noted the unconscious bodies in the corner, the lady with the hatpin, the giant of a man with fists the size of hatboxes. They were all panting for breath, and violence permeated the air. None of it mattered.

Only Summer.

She was pale, but her cheeks were red. She was as furious as she was frightened.

But she *was* frightened.

And for that alone, Tottenham would suffer.

"Let. Her. Go."

"I don't think so," Tottenham said, sealing his fate. "I did try to keep you out of it, my dear," he said to Summer. He had the gall to sound aggrieved. "You've been very kind to my granddaughter."

"April would not want her grandfather to be a murderer," Summer pointed out. Her neck was so vulnerable, the skin moving against the blade as she whispered. Too close—it was too close. Eliot advanced.

Tottenham tightened his hold on Summer's arm, twisting it behind her back. She yelped. Eliot froze. "Tottenham, don't. Just fucking don't."

"I'm doing this for April, you know," Tottenham told Summer as if they were chatting over tea. "She needs a dowry, an annuity to keep her safe. Her useless father certainly isn't up to the task. Anything might happen to her without an inheritance. Without protection. And I won't live forever."

"That is very true," Eliot said. "You framed Glass."

"He gambled away every stick of furniture, every candlestick that wasn't entailed."

"And you planted the note behind *The Red Mare* painting."

"Had to buy a painting no one else would buy, didn't I? Else he would have sold it too. He deserved it."

"But Lady Summer doesn't," Eliot said, trying to stay calm. She was right there, so close and yet so far out of reach. In *danger.*

"She's in a room full of spies, Blackpool," Tottenham said. "She can't be that innocent."

"Take me instead."

"She'll get me out of here far better than you could," he replied. "My April will have her safety. None of you will stop me."

"No one is going to hurt April," Summer said. "But there's no way out of here—you must see that."

"Enough of this. Burn the bloody door down."

"You'll kill us all," Lady Cole protested.

"Window's open," Tottenham said, backing toward it, Summer still in his grip. "Smoke will clear."

"There will be men waiting on the other side of that door," Eliot said. "It won't do you any good."

If they got here in time.

If no one decided to take matters into their own hands.

If Tottenham did not do something drastic.

If, if, if.

Eliot did not like his chances of getting to the guard before Tottenham could hurt Summer. He did not like his chances of the others lending their assistance. He did not like any of this. He lifted the pistol from inside his coat and pointed it at the guard. "You are not burning us to death."

"Blackpool, I will cut her," Tottenham warned. "Apologies, my dear. Truly."

"Apology not accepted," Summer muttered.

"Climb out that window, Tottenham," Eliot suggested. "Leave the rest of us here. It's over."

"It's just begun, boy."

Eliot smiled, and he knew it was sharp and vicious on his face.

"I don't think so, Tottenham. We broke your code. Your cipher was simple enough, once I knew you'd chosen *Debrett's*. And old version, at that. I admit, that part of it could have kept us chasing our tails for a while."

Tottenham paled.

"But we translated your list and have everyone safely away. Who would pay you for useless intelligence? May as well cut your losses."

Tottenham looked uncertain for the first time since Eliot had crashed into the room. He yanked Summer to the window and leaned out slightly to see how far down it was, no doubt wondering if he could climb to safety. Or jump.

He did not think to look up.

A small, very ornately framed painting of a pineapple fell from the roof and caught him on the back of the head.

Chapter Twenty-Seven

LORD TOTTENHAM MADE one very choked exclamation of pain before crumpling, unconscious. He landed with an audible thunk. Eliot had already leapt forward to grab the knife away from Summer as Tottenham fell, blood matting his hair. He shoved Summer behind him, pistol aimed at the guard once more. "Open the damn door."

"It's locked, mate."

Eliot whistled once, piercingly loud.

The door opened from the outside. Several men waited with weapons drawn, Beatrix a still, silent presence in their center. "You summoned?"

A tall, red-headed, and bearded man strolled into the parlor. "I got your gift, Blackpool. He was quite cross."

"You're welcome, Aidan," Eliot replied, not taking his eyes off Summer. He tilted her chin up to inspect her throat, clenching his jaw. "You're hurt."

"I'm not." She smiled. It was a bit tremulous for her liking, but it was still a smile. For some reason, her teeth chattered.

"It's shock," Eliot murmured, running his big, warm hands up and down her arms.

"*Your* teeth aren't chattering."

"Every bone in my body is chattering." He brought his arms up to her shoulders, dragging his thumb over her pulse. "He didn't cut you. I *might* not kill him."

"That was a very dashing entrance."

"I try."

"I'm sorry to say that the ladies will write sonnets about it when they find out."

His lips quirked. "I wager there will be even more sonnets about the undefeated Diamond of the Season."

Aidan paused in the act of dragging Tottenham away. "Are you wagering? At a time like this?"

Eliot laid his forehead against Summer's for a moment. "Always."

She wanted to lean into him more than she wanted anything else. But there was a crowd milling around them, taking the others into custody. Beatrix watched them like a stern governess who knew your tricks before you did. "Take the servant stairs," she suggested. "You'll cause less of a stir."

One of the men paused. "But he's an earl. And that one's a viscount."

"That earl is a traitor who held Lady Summer at knifepoint," Eliot corrected him. "Feel free to drop him on his head. Repeatedly."

"One of the women got away," a younger agent said, panting, clearly having run back up at top speed. "She *bit* me."

"Veiled?" Summer asked.

"No, the other one."

"Lady Cole," she said. "She lives in Berkeley Square."

Aidan tossed her a grin. "Want a job, lass?"

She grinned back.

"How about a husband?" he added with a touch of a swagger.

"Get lost, Aidan," Eliot grumbled.

Aidan hefted Tottenham up and took him away, laughing.

Eliot could not stop touching her, fingertips on her arm, palm to the small of her back, his thigh against hers. "We're going to talk about locking yourself into a room with spies and traitors, Summer," he promised softly.

"I survived."

If anything, he went slightly gray at her choice of verbs.

She poked her head outside of the window, looking up. "Maggie, is that you?"

Maggie's face popped over the edge of the roof. "Did I kill him?"

"No."

"Oh. I guess that's for the best."

"Thank you."

"You're welcome—now hush before you give away my position."

Summer ducked back inside. "What happens now?"

"We take this lot in for questioning," Eliot said. "Tottenham's unlikely to be hanged, though it's possible. More likely deportation."

"Poor April. He was only trying to help her."

"I'm not about to feel sorry for the man." He rubbed his jaw. "They're going to want me to go in as well. Seeing as I was tricked by that bloody message."

"We all were," Summer pointed out. "Including the War Office. Shall I come too? I have something to say to them."

Something softened in the harsh line of his shoulders. "I'd prefer to keep you out of it." He leaned closer, his words for her alone. "It's best if the new Lark isn't connected, don't you think?"

She beamed. Just half an hour ago she'd feared for his life and then her own, and now she was light as whipped cream. "Good point."

"Did you just agree with me?"

"Well, you were right for once," she teased.

"That might be the most harrowing part of the whole evening."

"True. You are so seldom right."

"Minx." There was such tenderness in his eyes that she found it hard to stay still. She wanted to touch him. To be touched. "Shall I call for your carriage?"

"Whatever for?"

"To see you home?" He sounded as perplexed as she did, clearly for a different reason.

"I'm fine, just a bit shaken. Nothing a bit of crime can't cure."

He blinked at her. "Pardon? You don't *want* to go home?"

"Don't be ridiculous. We still have art to steal."

"YOU HAD ME worried for a moment," Beatrix murmured as she helped Summer back into her costume and mask.

"The knife gave me pause, I admit."

"Not that."

Summer tied the ribbon of her mask. "What then?"

"I thought you might want to go home and drink tea and rest." Beatrix sounded like it was akin to stealing from an orphanage. "Er, though, of course, if you needed that, it would be fine. Understandable. No judgment."

Summer laughed. "This is the most tongue-tied I have ever seen you. Including the time Maggie tried to teach you to hang from her silks and you landed on your head."

"I only meant—"

Summer patted her arm. "I know what you meant. But this is our best chance to finish the job."

Beatrix deflated. "Oh, thank God. You know I can't abide loose ends."

"I know." They started down the main staircase, joining the entertainment still in full swing. The contrast was a little disorienting. "But you could have finished it without me."

"Not nearly as well."

Summer felt the last of the jagged energy tightening in her chest dissipate. "Beatrix, you would make a great lark."

"I know."

"Is that a yes?"

"Well, you can't do it all by yourself, can you?" Beatrix asked as if the answer was obvious. "Now, come along."

Summer accepted a glass of champagne and a passing compliment. She mingled with half-drunk guests dressed like birds and butterflies and flowers. She located the last two paintings that belonged to Aunt Georgie, and a sculpture of a laughing hippopotamus. The hippopotamus was the easiest to steal. It fit right in Aunt Georgie's hand, and she giggled all the way back to her carriage and right into the Rose House drawing room.

Meanwhile, Summer requested that the musicians play something jaunty and dramatic.

She had learned well to hide in plain sight. She stood in the center of the conservatory-turned-ballroom and pointed up to the skylight with a gasp. Conversations nearest to her faltered first, then the pause spread, returning on a wave of whispers.

The window opened and Maggie descended from the darkness, wrapped in her silks, dressed in her Astley's costume. Someone squeaked when she dropped suddenly, then hovered as if she had wings. She rolled, twisting and somersaulting, drawing everyone's interest. She rolled back and forth like a clock's pendulum, stretching her toes to grip a painting. In a feat of strength, she lifted it from the wall, dropped so that she was vertical, winked at someone from the royal family, and launched it right out of the open window.

Gasps and applause broke out. She managed an upside-down bow before swinging to the next painting.

"Oh, how clever," Summer exclaimed.

No one questioned it. Not the guests, not even the members of the Mayfair Art Collectors Society, who, to a man, thought the others had planned the entertainment.

Three paintings disappeared into the sky.

Aunt Georgie's collection had been reclaimed.

"THERE YOU ARE," Eliot said sometime later from the shadows of her bedroom where he waited. A single candle burned, and the balcony doors were open to the night breezes. He was unbearably handsome. Lean and lethal and so much more than everyone gave him credit for.

"Here I am."

"I beat you back here," he said, stepping forward. He was in his lawn shirt, cravat abandoned, sleeves rolled back. "You know what that means."

"I do?"

"I won our wager," he said, half smiling but eyes positively searing into her. He dug his fingers into the hair at her nape and tugged gently. She all but purred. "You have to marry me now. It's only fair."

"We can't get married on a dare." Her indignant tone was somewhat compromised by the purr and the fact that her eyes started to close of their own volition.

"We can do whatever we like," he disagreed.

"I won't stop being a lark."

"As I am not an imbecile, I had not considered that you would." His lips touched her throat.

"And you would want a wife who is a spy?" she asked incredulously, fighting the hope that warmed her as deeply as his kiss.

"I want *you* for a wife," he insisted. "You are clever and caring and bold. Even if you are rather plain."

She pinched him.

He smiled against her cheek. "Ugly, even."

His lips found hers, claimed her in a deep kiss that curled her toes in her dancing slippers. The candlelight reflected off the hundreds of silver spangles of her dress, like fairy lights. It pooled around her feet when he unhooked it. Her stays followed.

"I won't pretend my heart didn't stop when I saw the knife. Or the pistol in Aunt Georgie's drawing room. I fucking hate the thought of you in danger. I also fucking hate the thought of you unhappy. You don't need to be protected from yourself. You know who you are. But I won't stop protecting you from the world."

"Eliot." She nearly melted, right then and there.

"I love you, Summer. I've always loved you. Ever since you trounced me at chess that one time."

"*Three* times."

Under his thumb, her nipple pressed against the thin muslin of her chemise. He sucked it into his mouth, all while stalking her backward until her back touched the strawberry-patterned wall. He kissed her fiercely until her head began to swim. She clutched at his arms, his lean, muscular back. There was nothing but his mouth. "Marry me. Be my countess. My plum. Be happy with me. I dare you."

She nipped at his lower lip as he pressed into her. "Well, when you put in that way…"

"No quarter?"

"No quarter."

Epilogue

Christmas, later that year

T HE BLACKPOOL CARRIAGE, decorated with swaths of pine and holly, pulled up to a Mayfair house bright with candlelight and cheer. Eliot tugged Summer closer, nuzzling behind her ear. Her eyelids fluttered. "Don't start."

"I never stopped."

"True."

He teased her with a hard kiss, a soft stroke of his fingers up to her knee, drawing it up over his thighs. "Why do you think I had this new carriage built to be so spacious?"

"We do seem to have a thing for carriages." She sighed.

"It's the only place I get you all to myself."

They had married that summer but never quite got around to leaving Aunt Georgie's house until autumn, and even then it was only across the street. Beatrix never left, staying as a companion and a lark. Maggie joined when she could, but she preferred the circus ring.

It was Aunt Georgie who put them all to shame. No one looked twice at an old woman, even a Dowager Countess. And more importantly, no one *thought* twice if they noticed Aunt Georgie doing something odd or wandering where she wasn't meant to be wandering. She had found her calling as a spymaster.

Lord Glass, on the other hand, though cleared of charges of espionage and treason, fled to Italy in order to escape his creditors. April had stayed behind with Lady Susan, who clucked around her like a ferocious mother hen.

Summer gasped when Eliot suddenly sucked at her throat, soothing her with a tiny lick. "You smell like oranges," he drawled. "And you know I love oranges."

"We are expected."

"They'll have you all evening," he growled. "They can wait."

It was hard to argue with the languid heat that rose with the touch of his hand, mostly because she did not want to. Her back arched as his wicked fingers slid deep and he growled again, softer. "Come for me, plum."

"You first," she panted, gripping him tighter.

"Always a competition." He grinned. "But I'm going to win this time."

He dragged her wetness up through her sensitive folds and circled her bud, once, twice. Another finger slid deep, filling her. Her back arched off the seat as she gasped. He closed his teeth around her earlobe, breath ragged and sharp. "Come on," he urged. "I dare you."

She came apart with tiny mewling sounds; pleasure rushed up her thighs and spread outward. Trembles followed the honeyed aftershocks.

"I win," he murmured.

"I think I win, actually."

"When you make those noises, plum, I am always the winner."

"You are incorrigible," she scolded, quite happily. "But they are expecting a charming rake and the belle of the ball," she continued, putting her skirts to right. "Let's not disappoint them."

"You're armed?"

"I practically clatter and clank when I walk."

"And you're clear on the plan?" There was a thread of warning to his question. It never failed to heat her blood.

"Of course." She had delivered messages across London for months now, while Eliot was finally invited to concentrate on code breaking.

"Last week I had to fetch you from the Serpentine where you had become stuck in the ice, dear heart."

"All part of my plan."

"Not a lot of French spies dawdling in the ice," Eliot returned drily.

"Ha. Shows what you know. The ambassador's wife was so embarrassed that her dog pushed me into the icy waters that she invited me to tea, did she not?"

"She did."

Summer nodded smugly. "Just so."

"I'm surprised that no one has sent word to Bonaparte advising him to just give up now that you are involved."

Summer grinned. "It would be easier. He's not very amenable, is he? Appalling manners."

"I'll be sure to add it to the letter."

"Please do."

She snuggled into his warmth for a moment, savoring the cocoon of velvet and pine-scented air. "Eliot?"

"Yes?"

"I love you."

"I love *you*, you absolute menace. Now go on." He kissed her temple. "Shine."

About the Author

Alyxandra Harvey lives in an old stone house with her husband, multiple dogs, and a few resident ghosts who are allowed to stay as long as they keep company manners. She likes chai lattes, tattoos, and books. Sometimes fueled by literary rage.

Author of The Drake Chronicles, The Witches of London, Haunting Violet, Red, Love Me Love Me Not.

Twitter: AlyxandraH
Instagram: alyxandraharveyauthor

Milton Keynes UK
Ingram Content Group UK Ltd.
UKHW030016010324
438562UK00014B/406